Tommy's Tea Shack Tales

Tommy's Tea Shack Tales

M. T. Wells

ISBN 9798673267844

Contents

About the Author:

MT Wells was a contractor on the North Sea oil and gas platforms, initially working as a rope access and NDT technician in the UK northern sectors flying out of Aberdeen. After three years, he was asked to complete a two-week trip on a gas platform in the southern North Sea; 16 years later he was still there and had progressed to become an Offshore Inspection Engineer, managing teams of multi-skilled NDT technicians responsible for the asset integrity of 27 Normally Unmanned Installations. These platforms and assets have all now been decommissioned, and MT Wells has long since left the offshore life behind. He is now working from home in the North of England as a health and safety consultant to industry across the UK.

<u>Acknowledgements</u>

The idea for this book was the result of a good night out and a few beers with friends. A couple of good stories were told, and the seed was planted. So, to my wife, Susan, Richard and Lorraine, you are all to blame for this little project.

I had the pleasure of chatting to a lot of people when compiling the stories for this book, including current and past workmates as well as a few of the old guard who have long since retired.

I found that most guys didn't come out with a tale straight away. They often said they'd need to think about it as nothing sprang to mind, but then a day or two later, they would reel off a career's worth of stories, and the laughs would all come flooding back.

I'd like to thank the following for their tales and for helping to make the 'research' so easy. I would also add that the names below aren't necessarily directly involved. They may have simply been in the tea shack or on an inbetweenie when they heard someone say "You won't fucking believe this one…"

A huge thanks to Ryan C, Scott W, Shane H, Richard T, Dan C, Doug F, Phil P, Jeff O, Harry R, Stew M, Guy S, Danny R, Scott McG, Jim McC, Paul C, Micky G, John S, Ian M and Ron A. My days of walking into an offshore tea shack and listening to all the banter are now behind me, but if our paths cross again… I'll buy you a pint!

Stay Safe!

"My family and friends will no doubt speculate as to which of these tales I was involved in as Tommy. Now that really would be telling! I would go as far to say that I have been seen on the odd occasion brandishing a fireman's axe, sporting a fine piece of seagull-adorned headwear and on the odd occasion administering flu vaccines."

MT Wells

In memory of those who have tragically lost their lives working offshore and sadly never made it onto that demob flight home.

May you rest in peace.

My amazing wife Susan,

I will always be thankful to an industry that allowed our paths to cross. it was the worst job in the world when I had to leave you, but the best when I stepped back through the door to a loving kiss and a cold beer.

xXx

To my daughter Emelye,

I'm ever aware of the time we lost as you were growing up and I was offshore, but also grateful that I got to share the full cross-section of your childhood whilst home on leave.

The Tea Shack

During a typical 12-hour shift offshore there is normally both a morning and afternoon tea break of around 30 mins each. Depending on the platform and catering budget, there would be hot breakfast rolls or cheese on toast served for the morning break and cake or biscuits served during the afternoon. The food is served in the tea shack, a room where the workers can come in and sit wearing their work boots and overalls.

During tea breaks, anything and everything is discussed from food to football and supervisors to super models. The topics of conversation have no bounds, and guys will be slagged off if they are in the room or not. You can be put on a pedestal one minute and shot down the next. It can be one of the funniest yet also most abusive places on the platform, and it all takes place during those two half-hour time slots.

Some of the funniest stories are told to some of the most receptive of audiences, people will butt in and hecklers will always want to be heard, but the laughs are many, and on a good day the tales can come thick and fast.

The following pages in this book are memories of some of those tales, stories from the past. Like all good stories, they tend to mature over time as snippets are added and some bits are glossed over, but in general the truth always shines through.

For this book, those implicated in the tales are referred to as Tommy, an anonymity not given in the tea shack as the main aim of telling the story was generally to humiliate, single out or shoot down those involved.

The offshore world is a unique one with systems, practices and a way of life that differs so much from the general population who go about their nine-to-five working day. For that reason, each chapter starts with a little insight into an aspect of the coming tale to familiarise you with the life of an offshore worker.

The Inbetweenie

It's often the case that you can pass by the tea shack and see guys sneaking in a quick brew outside of tea-break times. This is known as the 'Inbetweenie', or if challenged by management it's a toolbox talk, pause for safety, permit delay or any other excuse you can think of.

Each tea shack tale throughout the book has an Inbetweenie or short tale tagged onto the end, and all of the tales within this book have been volunteered by some of the many guys who I have worked with over the years. There are, however, some stories that are best left out in the North Sea and not suitable for publication, as per the offshore motto:

Safety First!

CHAPTER 1

The Flight

Prior to flying to an offshore installation, the passengers (as with any flight) must first go through a standard check-in procedure. Typically, this involves having all bags weighed as well as being asked to step on the scales yourself. The total aircraft weight is required when calculating the fuel requirements and range, etc. In addition, the weather conditions must be taken into consideration to assess if the aircraft is potentially overweight. A fully loaded helicopter can struggle to gain lift when there is little or no wind. If deemed too heavy, then either passengers or baggage would be removed ('bumped') from the flight to ensure that the aircraft can operate safely on the intended route.

The next stage is the security check. As with commercial passenger aircraft, all baggage is scanned; however, for offshore flights an additional physical check of the contents is made by airport security prior to the bags being transported to the helicopter for loading. The passengers are then taken to a briefing room where they watch a video which outlines the safety features of the helicopter and actions to be taken in the unlikely event of an emergency.

The final stage is where things get very different to your average holiday flight. The passengers are issued with a survival suit, essentially a dry suit which along with the user's clothes forms an insulating barrier from the cold seawater extending the survival time should they have to evacuate into the sea after a ditching. In addition, passengers also don a lifejacket, the modern versions of which have an integrated Personal Locator Beacon (PLB) and an Emergency Breathing System (EBS) which essentially is a scaled-down version of the Self-Contained Underwater Breathing Apparatus (SCUBA) used by recreational divers. The EBS provides breathing air when submerged should the aircraft capsize or take on water to aid an underwater escape through a door or window opening.

From here they board the aircraft for the flight where they secure themselves with a four-point harness and sit shoulder to shoulder very crammed against their often newly acquainted travelling companions for what can feel like an exceptionally long and uncomfortable journey.

Teatime Teaser

Apprentice: "I'm not sure I can climb the derrick. I'm scared of heights."

Toolpusher: "The chopper was at 2,000 feet when it flew out here, or did you swim, son? Now put a fucking harness on and get up that ladder!"

Tommy's Tale

Tommy had arrived in Aberdeen for his flight in good time. He wasn't due to check in until 9am the following day but chose to arrive the day before and spend the night in one of the fine local B&Bs in Dyce using his travel allowance of £120. Tommy wasn't stupid, he knew he could drive his car there, pick up one of his work mates en route and rip him off for a few quid petrol money. He also knew a section of road where the double yellow lines had been covered by new tarmac during road repairs, and he could abandon his battered car there for next two weeks, avoiding the airport parking charges, but sadly not the 14 days of seagull crap that his car seemed to attract.

Once settled into his room (open the door, ditch the off-shore bags and leave the room), he headed downstairs to meet his mate to go out for a curry and a couple of beers. It had been a long day and he was ready for a pint and a belly full of food before heading back to the digs for the monthly sleepless night in the damp-filled room that was lit by the amber streetlight through the paper-thin curtains. He also knew the mattress had more DNA on it than an episode of *CSI: Miami*, but again the additional savings made by not staying at one of the larger mainstream hotels made enduring a restless night worthwhile.

For some reason, Tommy opted for a change in routine when he selected his curry, the usual dopiaza and mushroom rice was replaced by a seafood special with spicy sauce, signified by the five small chilli icons on the menu. When the meal arrived, even the waiter had to step in and offer reassurance as his mate took the piss from behind his sensible chicken korma. "Ya fanny," Tommy thought as he tucked in with his not-so-asbestos mouth. It took a while to get through, but he accepted the challenge laid down by his own ego and cleaned the plate, job done!

The next morning, the alarm went off and they headed straight to the heliport by taxi, again avoiding the added extra charges of a cooked breakfast. Typically, a coffee whilst they waited for the flight was enough to last them until they got to the rig and headed straight for an early lunch, essentially a free all-you-can-eat buffet!

Things for Tommy didn't quite seem right. He had that pit of the stomach feeling that he needed the loo, but something told him that he wasn't going to get to choose when that would be. He also knew what was simmering within, and if his breath was anything to go by, it wasn't going to be pretty when the inevitable did happen. Still, no need to panic, he thought, as there was at least an hour for things to come good whilst they waited for the flight and went through the check-in procedure.

To everyone's surprise, the flight was called earlier than expected, and Tommy, his mate and the rest of the guys made their way to check-in. Tommy hopped on the scales, and the lads joked with the check-in girl hinting that she should knock a kilo or two off as he'd soon be shedding some weight. During the safety video, Tommy had a minor gas release as a precursor of things to come. On the plus side, it silenced the other 15 guys, who were trapped within the confines of the briefing room, and Tommy took some pleasure in watching them gag.

Just as Tommy was about to go and pay a call, the ground crew announced that the flight would be lifting early and that all passengers were to suit up (don their survival suits and lifejackets) and wait to board the aircraft.

Tommy simply couldn't wait any longer. He stole away from the room and legged it towards the two toilets. One was out of order and the other occupied. He was also followed by a pissed-off member of the ground staff, who told him to get suited up or risk being bumped from the flight.

Within no time at all, he was trapped. Suited up and on the aircraft with one arse cheek clinging to the seat as the guy next to him must have been pushing the 150kg mark and was taking up the one and half seats that he obviously thought his arse was entitled to. It must have been the added strain of trying to hold off Jabba the Hutt, who was leaning against him, that triggered Tommy's first in-flight fart. Now the thing with farting in a survival suit is that nobody else notices as it can't be heard above the drone of the helicopter rotors and it often can't be smelt as you are pretty much vacuum packed by a neoprene sealed, waterproof suit. The interesting thing, however, is that the smell remains as fresh as the moment it was packed and waits ready to be released the moment you unzip the suit on arrival at the platform. Often 16 such farts can be released from a flight of passengers all at the same time, quite an achievement!

For Tommy, though, things got a whole lot worse as without any warning his stomach cramped and the fermented spicy seafood special unloaded into his underwear. With only five minutes to run until landing on the platform, Tommy sat and felt the vacuum action of his survival suit force the soiled delights of the night before up the small of his back. This was a smell that couldn't be contained within the suit and it slowly permeated into the tightly packed cabin. At one point, it even got the attention of the captain, who turned with disgust to his passengers as his co-pilot manoeuvred the aircraft, now on final approach to the platform helideck.

Once landed, they disembarked and made their way into heli-admin (the small arrivals room), where you remove your survival suit and are allocated a cabin for the duration of your stay. At this point, everyone was commenting on the smell, the smell that didn't do the fart thing and go away once its job was done. The smell was just getting worse and as all but one of the passengers had removed their suits it soon became apparent where the smell was coming from.

There he was, standing isolated in a room full of people highlighted by a bright yellow survival suit when the female medic running the heli-admin asked the question. "Excuse me, are you going to take your survival suit off?" Tommy's shoulders slumped as he replied "No love, I've just shit myself!"

For Tommy, the next two weeks offshore were to be the longest of his career.

Inbetweenie

"I watched a guy taunt the chef as he went down the counter loading his plate up with food. 'The beef looks tough again!' and 'How do you put the lumps in the mashed carrots?' and 'This gravy looks as thick as fuck!'

The chef's eyes followed him all the way to his table and didn't look away until he saw him take his first mouthful, which was immediately spat back onto the plate, by which time the chef had made his way over to his table and was looking down at him. He'd covered his Sunday roast in the hot chocolate sauce for the desserts rather than the gravy.

'Thick as fuck, eh? Is that the gravy or you son?'"

CHAPTER 2

The Cabin

In general, a cabin consists of two single side-by-side beds or a bunk bed. Each bed has a blackout curtain that can be drawn for privacy and a reading light. The cabin would normally also have a television that the occupants share via a single remote control, and some platforms also provide satellite television as well as a separate DVD player.

For storage, there tends to be four lockers, two for the current occupants and two that are secured by the workers who are on leave. This extra storage allows the regular crew members to leave items offshore and avoid flying additional baggage to and from the platform every month. The cabin normally is equipped with an en-suite toilet, shower and sink with little room for anything else.

Most rooms also have a grab bag or emergency bag containing a smoke hood, torch and gloves. The smoke hood extends the survival time in a smoke-filled atmosphere providing filtrated air for the user, the gloves are to protect against hot and sharp surfaces in the event of a fire or explosion and the torch is for visibility should there be a loss of emergency lighting.

Some cabins will have a window with a sea view; however, the double glazing has a larger void than that in your standard household windows. The outer bulkheads are constructed to ensure blast and heat protection can be maintained for as long as possible following an explosion or during a fire, and as such the void between the inner and outer glass can be up to half a metre thick.

Teatime Teaser

Young visitor to the rig and temporary cabin user: "I'll be in the recreation room whilst you grab a shower and sort yourself out. How will I know when the cabin is free for me to come in?"

Heavily tattooed Geordie welder and permanent cabin user: "When I've finished, I'll leave the door slightly open. Until then, don't come in!"

He then closes the door, switches the light off and goes to sleep.

Young lad spends the night in the rec room, too scared to enter.

Tommy's Tale

Tommy had arrived on the rig for what was to be his third offshore trip although it was his first time on this platform. He'd completed his first two offshore trips out of Aberdeen so was starting to feel confident with the travel to the airport, the check-in process and the flight offshore. For this trip, he would be on a new team. He had already met the other two guys at the heliport and felt at ease with them straight away. Two weeks offshore with guys you are clearly not going to get on with can be a very long and painful experience as you not only have to endure a 12-hour shift with them but potentially share a cabin together as well.

Tommy and the other newly arrived passengers formed a queue at the counter within heli-admin where the platform medic behind the desk was allocating cabins. Each new arrival handed over their Vantage card (ID and offshore tracking card), and it was in turn displayed on the large board on the wall indicating their allotted cabin number and which bunk they were in, top or bottom. Tommy soon realised that his two teammates had been assigned a cabin to share and that he was given a bottom bunk in another cabin. He could see there was a card already displayed against the top bunk.

Both Tommy's colleagues noticed that he had a bottom bunk and instantly tore into him for getting the golden ticket on his first trip to the platform. Tommy overheard one of them say "He's got stranger danger!" as he strained his eyes to see if he could get a gauge on the guy he'd be sharing with by the blurred photo on his Vantage card in the slot for the top bunk.

As with all new arrivals, Tommy had to be guided through a platform induction and spent the rest of the shift being shown around the rig by the safety advisor and in turn had a 'green hat' talk by the platform Offshore Installation Manager (OIM). Most platforms have a policy where new starts must wear a green hard hat on site to highlight to others that they are new to the installation and may require assistance in an emergency or just general guidance throughout the working day. The OIM is primarily responsible for the health, safety and welfare of everybody on his installation and as such has a little welcome chat with all new personnel to outline the safety culture on board. Tommy recalled his last OIM brief and wondered if they were all trained to give the same speech at OIM school as he wasn't hearing anything different this time around.

With all the formalities complete, the shift was over and Tommy headed back to the cabin to unpack his bags and get settled in. He could see that all the lockers were padlocked and in use, even the one clearly marked 'Visitor Locker Only'.

"Bollocks!" he thought, "I guess I'll be living out of my bag then."

He took his toiletries out of his kit bag and stepped into the small toilet/shower area connected to the room where there was a metal bathroom cabinet on the wall. He picked up his shower gel, deodorant and shaving foam to place them on the bottom shelf. He could see his roommate had already taken the top shelf (as he was in the top bunk) and filled it with his toiletries: a very tired-looking toothbrush, a Bic razor and bar of Imperial Leather soap.

"Do people actually still use Imperial Leather?" Tommy thought as he sized up his tins and shower gel, soon realizing none of them would fit on the small bottom shelf. Back in the bag they went!

Dinner time came, and Tommy met his two colleagues on the way down to the galley, where they were served food by a stewardess, who was smartly dressed in her white top and paper hat. Tommy gazed down at the hotplate and was impressed by the selection on the menu. He glanced up at the stewardess and was about to ask for his dish of choice when he read the penned message on the rim of her paper hat. '7 foot of cock on this rig and I can't get 7 inches!'…

"Erm, I'll have the Polish sausage, please," Tommy muttered, his work mates sniggering as they made their way to the table.

After dinner, Tommy headed up to the cabin, where he kicked off his shoes and stretched out on the bed. In no time at all, he was out cold; the day had taken its toll. Unbeknownst to him, when he entered the cabin, his roomy was already in the toilet and about to have a shower. When Tommy nodded off, the shower went on but he continued to sleep, only being woken by the sound of Mr Stranger Danger urinating into the toilet like a shire horse in full flow. The toilet flushed and Tommy sat bolt upright on his bed against the fixed ladder that led to the top bunk, ready to introduce himself.

There is an unwritten rule on the rigs that you agree on a routine at the end of the day to allow your cabin mate time to shower and change in peace. When they are done, they then tip you off and you head up for your own bit of free space. Tommy had broken this rule and was sat on his bed at the exact time that his roomy stepped bollock naked into the centre of the cabin, his 'bits' dangling at Tommy's eye level. This was to be their initial introduction to one another, but Tommy chose not to extend his hand.

"Don't mind me, son!" said the six-foot-five Yorkshire scaffolder as he placed his foot on the bottom rung of the ladder and swung his other leg up to mount the top bunk. Tommy just sat there frozen in shock as the naked lump of a man scaled the ladder that he was still leaning against, his hairy arse dangerously close as it went past his face. The gap between the top of the ladder and the ceiling is quite tight, making the mattress-mounting manoeuvre quite an awkward one. This time the forward-facing entry was the chosen technique, which meant having to lean in whilst cocking one leg up onto the bed. Having just finished emptying his bladder over the toilet moments before, the action of climbing into the bunk had released the last few drips of urine and just as Tommy was about to stand and leave the droplets splashed onto his nose and cheek.

The unwritten rule of giving your roommate some space was one that Tommy would never forget.

Inbetweenie

"We were working on a Normally Unmanned Installation (NUI) for the day. There were six of us on board including the OIM. The manager that day was a company man through and through, so we were all surprised when he announced that as it was such a red-hot day it seemed a shame to sit inside for our break. 'I'm heading outside for a spot of sunbathing,' he declared as he left the control room taking a chair with him. I noticed he had started to unzip his overalls on the way out and take off his hard hat. Given the PPE policy offshore I couldn't believe my luck. I stripped off to my boxer shorts and rigger boots and grabbed one of the thin overnight mattresses that were used if ever we were stranded on board overnight. I strutted out onto the main deck like a surfer with his longboard under his arm striding onto the beach. As I turned the corner the OIM was sat there with his helmet on his lap, overalls zipped up and not an inch of skin showing apart from his face and hands.

In contrast I was stood right in front of him in my boxer shorts and boots and no excuses!"

CHAPTER 3

Offshore Weather

The weather offshore can be extremely harsh and have an adverse effect on day-to-day operations. Extreme winds can make working in exposed areas very dangerous; high wind speeds can stop crane operations, close helidecks and prevent working at height. Rough seas can stop boat operations such as diesel or freshwater bunkering (re-supply). Standby vessels provide close standby (rescue cover) during helicopter operations or if scaffolders or Rope Access Technicians (RATs) are working at height with a potential to fall to sea. If the skipper of the vessel deems that the sea state is too high to launch his Fast Rescue Craft (FRC) and provide rescue cover, then such operations will be suspended. If the platform is shrouded in fog, then all flying programmes can be ceased if the cloud base is deemed too low for safe flying. During such times, the fog horn will sound with two short tones and one long one to warn vessels in the area. This will continue day and night until the visibility improves. Storms can remain over a platform for a few days, and fog banks have been known to shroud offshore platforms

17

for weeks.

In addition to the impact on business, this also hampers workers who are due to fly home on completion of their shift. Each day of cancelled flying would be an added day onto your trip as well stealing a day from your leave.

Teatime Teaser

Young scaffolder being assessed by his supervisor: "I'm going to come down, mate. It's pissing it down and I'm getting soaked up here!"

Glaswegian scaff foreman: "Aye, ney bother, son, get yersel' down and let's get you sorted out!"

Relieved young lad steps down onto the deck and is handed a rag by his sympathetic boss.

Foreman: "Now dry your eyes, sweet cheeks, and get the fuck back up there!"

Tommy's Tale

It had been a remarkably busy trip for Tommy but also a successful one. He was quite new to the offshore world, but as a graduate engineer he felt he had a good understanding of the process and operations from his training onshore and just needed to gain more practical experience before taking on a Team Leader (TL) role within his group. The guys he was working with were all older and highly experienced mechanics, electricians and technicians with a wealth of knowledge on tap, which Tommy was soaking up like a sponge. From day one offshore, Tommy had decided to get stuck in and learn the job from the ground up. He was always first to lend a hand and keen to be able to help and in turn learn along the way.

The trip was coming to an end, and the normal talk of the weather forecast raised its head. Twice a day, the platform would receive an updated five-day weather forecast from the Met Office in Aberdeen. The forecast is specific to the block (area) that the platform is in offshore and predicts the wind speeds, wave heights and cloud base specific to that area for the coming days. The forecast is displayed for all to see, but regardless of this, a large portion of the guys due to go home turn into meteorologists and can be heard spouting their own 'They've got it all wrong again' weather reports. They refuse to believe any forecast that could scupper their flight off; even worse if flights are cancelled and the actual weather doesn't look that bad. When this happens, the meteorologists suddenly become qualified commercial helicopter pilots and are quick to point out how easy it is to fly in such conditions.

Choppers eve had arrived (the day before going home), but sadly so too had the fog horn, and its long drawn-out drone was rumbling through the accommodation as Tommy and the team were sat having a cuppa before heading down for the morning meeting. After the meeting, Tommy was asked to report to the platform control room as they had a task that they wanted him to carry out. As with all such requests, Tommy was as keen as ever to help.

The Control Room Operator managed to keep a straight face as he explained to Tommy that fog samples were required for analysis. He went on to explain the procedure. Once briefed, Tommy took the sample bags (bin liners) and headed up to the helideck, where he performed what could only be described as a dance, almost waltz-type steps, scooping the air into the bin bags, which he then tied closed to secure the samples.

Now Tommy did think he must look pretty stupid but took comfort in the fact that he was alone on the helideck out of sight of the other platform personnel, and it was obviously a priority task and yet more valuable experience for him.

Once he had completed it, Tommy headed back to the control room with his two bin liners of fog. He was feeling pleased with himself as he'd got his head around yet another one of the many offshore procedures. The smile soon turned to utter embarrassment as he stepped into the control room and was greeted by a massive cheer and piss-taking taunts. All his team were in there, and most of the platform operators and supervisors; in fact, pretty much the whole shift had crammed into the small control room to watch the monitor on the wall that displayed the helideck video feed of the gullible engineer prancing around trying to catch clouds.

The fog cleared later that day, allowing Tommy and his team to fly off as planned for their much-needed leave.

Tommy's fog samples were no longer required, but the tale of his actions followed him throughout the rest of his offshore career.

Inbetweenie

"There was a sticker on the mirror in the shower which read, 'The sensors in this cabin are extremely sensitive, ensure the door to the shower is closed when spraying aerosols'. I, however, learnt the hard way when I stepped out of the bathroom into the cabin and proceeded to spray on deodorant. Instantly, the alarms went off with a tannoy stating they had a fire indication in the accommodation and all personnel report to their muster stations immediately. It was late at night and I had been to the gym. I arrived at muster to see 75 extremely pissed-off guys who had been dragged out of bed whilst I stood there as fresh as a daisy. The fire team were deployed to investigate the alarm, and the indication light above my cabin door singled me out as the culprit.

I was named and shamed over the tannoy system for all to hear and it was a long walk back to my cabin surrounded by a crew of highly pissed off guys."

CHAPTER 4

Rope Access

The offshore platforms are immense with some structures towering hundreds of metres above sea level. Troll A platform was the tallest and heaviest structure to be moved on earth during its transit to the Troll Gas Field off the west coast of Norway. The platforms are fully equipped with various types of process plant, pipework, pressure vessels, communication and electrical systems and so much more, all of which require maintenance and frequent inspections.

To work at height and often over the sea various techniques can be utilised, the two most common being scaffolding to erect a safe working platform and rope access as a more flexible and temporary approach. Rope access historically derives from a combination of both caving and climbing techniques but at a much safer, controlled and industrial level. Offshore rope access in the UK is governed by the Industrial Rope Access Trade Association (IRATA), which over the years has continued to develop a safe system of work in accordance with UK and European legislation. Rope Access Technicians, often referred to as abseilers or rope techs, are trained to three main levels of competency, the most senior being the rope access level 3 technician, who is the safety supervisor and most often Team Leader. Teams can vary in size but typically will consist of two or three technicians when operating offshore depending on the nature of the work.

All Rope Access Technicians are trained in various methods of access and rescue techniques depending on their IRATA qualification or level. Rope access is, however, merely the means to access the workplace, and as such they all generally have additional trade qualifications such as being an electrician, painter, inspector or welder.

Teatime Teaser

OIM to the rope access Team Leader: "Right, guys, we are going to have the boat in at 2am, so I'll need you guys over the side around midnight."

Rope access Team Leader: "Sorry, but we can't work over the sea at night due to Search and Rescue restrictions in the dark."

OIM: "You'll be around 80 metres above the sea, a fall from there and you're dead! In which case, we'll just wait for sunrise to recover your bodies in the morning after breakfast. Now are you working for us, or am I booking you on the next flight off?"

Tommy's Tale

During the morning meeting, it was announced that the visit of a Very Important Person (VIP) from Houston to the platform was likely to be postponed and that all planned work activities were to go ahead as normal. For Tommy and the other two guys on the rope access inspection team this meant they would be continuing with their visual inspections of the structural supports on the underside of the main deck.

It took a while to get all the required signatures and approvals in place on the permit, but after a couple of hours of tracking down management all the paperwork was signed off and good to go. It turned out that the VIP, a corporate safety executive from the States, had arrived on the morning flight just after the meeting, throwing the platform into bit of a flap. The rope access team headed out to do a final check of the worksite and erect chain barriers on the deck below to create an exclusion zone and prevent people from any potential dropped objects that could fall and ruin their day. The three-man team were all kitted up in full harnesses with two ropes rigged over the side of the platform. One of the key areas of the IRATA safe system of work is that all rope access systems have a double rope and anchor set up. This ensures that there is always a backup rope should one fail or snap, and in turn there is a backup anchor point should one of the wire strops to which the ropes are attached fail. As per the rescue plan, the level 3 supervisor had rigged the ropes using a system that allowed the technician working on them to be lowered to the deck below in the event of an emergency; there was also the option to haul him back onto the main deck should he become incapacitated or injured.

As the level 1 technician, Tommy was going to be the man making the short abseil of only a couple of metres, just enough for him to lean back underneath the structure and photograph the steelwork for his report. In the highly unlikely event that he was to fall, there was the potential for him to bounce from the deck 12 metres below and land in the sea, an additional 25-metre drop. As this was therefore classed as 'working over the side', in addition to his harness he was also wearing a self-inflating lifejacket with a personal locator beacon attached.

The Team Leader (TL) fired the handheld radio into life and notified the boat of their intentions. "Hello, skipper, this is work party 1, we have one man about to work over the side on the north side of the main deck; we have two men on standby. Are you in position and OK for close standby cover? Over."

"Work party 1, that's all clear, we have your location, one man over the side and two men on standby. We have you covered."

"Over you go!" said the TL as Tommy connected his descender and backup device to the ropes and clambered over the handrail. He was soon over the side and had lowered himself into position. He spun himself around so that the upper part of his body was out of sight under the main deck and just his legs were sticking out in view of his TL.

During this manoeuvre, the VIP safety executive from the

States appeared along with the OIM and the platform safety advisor. They got the attention of the TL, who gave them the thumbs-up to enter the barriered area for a chat. They then had a brief safety conversation with the third team member to gain an understanding of the task, potential hazards and what controls the team had in place. The TL had his eyes on Tommy and occasionally would speak to him to ensure he was OK, but his ears were tuned into the questions his teammate was getting bombarded with as any shoddy answers would reflect pretty poorly on him. He soon relaxed when he heard the replies being given, explaining the details of the rope system that could be lowered or raised. He also demonstrated good knowledge of the worksite pointing out the Emergency Shutdown (ESD) button, the nearest telephone, eye wash station and emergency shower. "Fuck me, I briefed these boys well" thought the TL as he heard the amazing feedback and big American slap on the back that was awarded.

The TL, however, didn't realise that when Tommy had spun himself under the large structural beam he had turned to be faced with the biggest fucking seagull known to man, but to his instant relief it was dead. Somehow it had found its final resting place to be on the sheltered ledge of the beam tucked under the structure.

Back on the main deck the impressed VIP and his entourage were just about to leave the guys to their work when Tommy, who had no idea of the visitors above had taken the seagull, stretched out its huge wings and secured it to the top of his climbing helmet using the elastic head torch strap, suddenly popped up and shouted, "Look at this fucker!!"

Instantly his face dropped when he saw the unexpected guests, the VIP and OIM looking straight at him as the head of the dead seagull flopped around as if it had seen the funny side and was having one last chuckle to itself.

Later that day, after the VIP had departed the platform, Tommy's name was bellowed out over the platform tannoy with an order to report to the OIM's office immediately!

Inbetweenie

"The new platform was fully commissioned and ready to start production; just the final finishing touches were being put in place. The tropical fish tanks were loaded with water and formed centre pieces to a few of the recreational areas and offices. The guy tasked with loading the fish into the various tanks was made aware that they had been delivered to the platform but wasn't sure which of the shipping containers they were in. He explained to the materials co-ordinator that they were individually packed in watertight containers that had outer polystyrene protection. The materials man went drip white; he'd handed the boxes marked 'fish' to the catering crew, who had naturally put them straight into the freezer!"

As an added bonus, there was a second order placed for

the tropical fish, which arrived on the alternate crew's rotation. They made exactly the same mistake and froze the lot!"

CHAPTER 5

Catering

If you were to think of the platform accommodation module as a hotel and the workforce as its guests, then like any hotel the Personnel On Board (POB) need catering for. Typically, the contract is awarded to one company, who provide the chefs, stewards and stewardesses who service the living quarters.

The galley (kitchen) will run as a 24-hour operation and would normally have a chef or baker on night shift preparing the breads and as much of the food as possible for the chefs due to start their day shift. The night baker would also cook the meals for the night shift and depending on shift times prepare the cooked breakfast for the platform day shift.

The stewards and stewardesses would have a multitude of tasks to complete during their 12-hour shift. These would include the cleaning of internal areas such as the cabins, toilet facilities and offices. They would also run the laundry, washing and drying the clothes for the entire POB overnight ready for them to wear the next day as well as the bedding and towels.

In addition, they would assist in the galley preparing for meals and cleaning the dishes, pans and cooking utensils after each serving.

The entire operation is managed by the Camp Boss, who is normally the head chef. He also manages the logistics and orders the shipping containers of fresh food and frozen produce as well as consumable items such as cleaning materials.

As with most offshore personnel, the catering crew also have dual roles in an emergency and will often also be trained as first aiders, fire crew, muster controllers or assist in running the heli-admin.

Teatime Teaser

Camp boss (head chef) to random new guy: "Did I just see you sit down and put salt on your food without even bothering to taste it?!? Do you know me?!? Have you ever tried my food before?!? Did you just assume that all of my food is served unseasoned?!?"

Random new guy: "I didn't… Err… I mean… Err."

Camp boss: "Ah fuck off! Why do I even bother!"

Tommy's Tale

It was early on Sunday morning, and the platform had just completed their weekly muster. It had gone well apart from the new guy who had reported to lifeboat 1 muster point when he should have been at lifeboat 2. The main thing, though, was that they had him accounted for, and when they contacted the Emergency Control Centre (ECC) with the head count, it matched the expected Personnel On Board (POB). There was a short test of the Prepare to Abandon Platform Alarm (PAPA), and all personnel were stood down to go about their duties.

Tommy was the muster man on lifeboat 1, so he collared the newbie stray and pointed out that as he was in a cabin with an even number, his lifeboat and muster point would be lifeboat 2. "It's not hard, is it?" Tommy said and shook his head as the green hat headed out to work having learnt his lesson. It was also driven home by the large collective sigh that was directed at him from the rest of the guys at lifeboat 1 when he had held his hand up and declared that his name hadn't been called out. They had all probably been there, but any opportunity to take the piss was always pounced upon.

Tommy had put the clipboard back on the shelf at the muster point and turned off the radio. He hung up his fluorescent bib jacket identifying him as the muster controller and headed back to level 2 of the accommodation to carry on with his daily routine of cleaning the cabins and stripping any beds where the occupant was due to depart the platform later that day.

There was a pipe-fitting job due to start the next day, and the two guys carrying out the task wanted to sit down and finalise the paperwork before submitting the permit. The guy who was going to be work leader on the permit suggested they head

31

to his cabin where they could sit in peace and double-check everything before handing it in for review. As they sat in the cabin, the TL noticed the rank smell of a fart, and as there was only the two of them in there it didn't take much working out who had let one slip. The other fitter instantly denied it, and they carried on working through the risk assessments. Some 20 minutes later, the accused was firing back at the TL, this time blaming him for the rank smell that filled the small cabin. Hearing the commotion, Tommy piped up from inside the cabin's toilet and apologised as he'd been caught short.

Tommy, who was cleaning the TL's cabin, had been overwhelmed by the call of nature, and rather than heading to his own room, just a few doors away, had opted to settle down on his crapper and unload. He heard the two guys enter the room and thought they would soon leave, so he just sat there deadly quiet. He later admitted that he had to pipe up when his legs started to go numb, and he realised that if he didn't wipe his arse, things would start to dry in place. As the red faced and embarrassed Tommy stepped into the room and apologised to the guy whose cabin it was, the green hat, who earlier had mistakenly mustered at lifeboat 1, glared at Tommy.

"Next time use your own toilet! It's not hard, is it!"

Inbetweenie

"Whilst the guys were killing time and sitting around in the office waiting for a job to start, they took advantage of a nearby computer to surf the net. One at a time, they would step away from the group and hop on the PC that was just around the corner. The last guy to go opened the internet browser and clicked on 'history' to look for the web address for the site he had visited earlier. He scanned the list and in disgust headed back to the guys demanding to know who the dirty fucker was that had been looking at 'He-Brides.com'. All of them denied it and asked him what the hell he was going on about.

'He-Brides,' he said. 'C'mon, who's just been on that pc looking at He-Brides; I'm not thick, ya know! It's there in the internet history!'

His demands for justice were quite vocal and attracted the attention of one of the managers, who naturally was keen to see who the accused was as he might need to intervene and take action, especially if there had been someone looking at things online that were against company policy. One of the lads soon realised what all of the confusion was about, and in his Scottish west coast accent declared 'I was just looking at a website from home about The Hebrides, if that helps!'

The manager then looked over at the 'prosecution'. 'So, you're not thick, eh? Really?'"

CHAPTER 6

Apprenticeships

The Oil and Gas Technical Apprentice Programme is managed by both OPITO – originally standing for Offshore Petroleum Industry Training Organisation and the Engineering Construction Industry Training Board (ECITB). The apprenticeship programmes are supported by the oil and gas operators and contractor companies. On completion of a college course, those on the scheme are given placements on an offshore platform or onshore asset to complete on-the-job training.

OPITO manage the programme on behalf of the operators or duty holders whilst the ECITB run the programme for the contracting companies. During the four-year apprenticeship period, the trainees are assigned a mentor to guide them through the process. A typical apprenticeship would involve a 21-month college education followed by a 24-month rotation on an offshore platform where they would gain the practical and technical knowledge and skills to achieve a vocational qualification.

On completion of the apprenticeship and provided there are employment vacancies available, those who have excelled will be offered a permanent position as part of the platform crew and begin a new career in the world of oil and gas.

Teatime Teaser

OIM: "Why have you got 'Shaky' embroidered as your name on your company overalls? What's your real name?"

Shaky: "It's the nickname given to me when I was in the navy. My real name is Simon."

OIM: "Then I shall be calling you Simon. You're not in the navy now!"

A few days later.

OIM: "It's about time you had a shave, Simon!"

Shaky: "No thanks, I'm not in the navy now!"

Tommy's Tale

Tommy was on an early lunch break as his next task had to be carried out during a quiet period on the platform to have minimal impact on the rest of the workforce. He was told to work through lunch when most of the guys would be in the accommodation module and not on the park. After grabbing an early bite to eat, he had gone back to his cabin and switched on his iPod to chill out to some music before going back to work.

He picked up his magazine and started thumbing through the pages. It wasn't exactly porn, but some of the photos and articles had got the blood flowing to the young man's loins. After a few minutes, standing there in the middle of the cabin, he gave no thought to where he was; he just dropped his trousers and took himself in hand with the ferocity of a jack hammer. "Yes, this is happening," he thought and he was loving it, that is, until he saw something move behind him in the reflection on the TV screen. He turned to see the back of the stewardess who had caught him in action and immediately spun around and left the room. The door to his cabin had closed, and so too, he thought, had the door to his career offshore, the career that he had barely begun. His previous joy turned to cold sweat, and his active imagination switched to trying to come up with a viable excuse. He sat on his bunk, head in hands trying to concoct a bullshit story, but without knowing exactly how much she had seen, he didn't have one.

Tommy opted to see if she was about and somehow offer up an apology, but as he walked down the corridor he spotted her leaving the OIM's office and disappearing into another office opposite. His heart started thumping as she must have headed straight there to report him. Making a split-second decision, he approached the OIM's door. All offices offshore have an open-door policy; if the door is closed, then that generally signifies a confidential chat or a meeting. The OIM's door was open and he was sitting at his desk tapping away at the computer keyboard, probably emailing Tommy's company regarding the incident that had just been brought to his attention.

Sheepishly, Tommy tapped on the open door to make his presence known to the OIM. He explained that he had bit of a sensitive problem, so the manager told him to close the door and take a seat. Tommy explained in as little detail as he could get away with what it was he'd been caught doing and that he knew that the stewardess had just been to see the OIM, so he wanted to hopefully clear the air and 'come clean' so to speak. The OIM sat stony-faced throughout, glaring straight at him, which just added to the young apprentice's worries. "So, you've been caught ripping the head off it, and you want me to make the whole thing go away?" said the OIM. In no uncertain terms Tommy was told to get on with his work that afternoon, and if by tea break he hadn't been summonsed, then for now, he could consider the matter closed, but he warned him that he hadn't heard the last of it. Tommy left the office, heart thumping, and hadn't felt that he'd achieved anything by his little confession. The OIM sat back in his chair, chuckled to himself and picked up the phone....

It was approaching three o'clock and Tommy was making his way across the bridge for his tea break. He took off his gloves, helmet and safety glasses and chucked them on the rack before making his way into the tea shack. The moment the door opened, there was a massive cheer and shouts of 'you wanker!' as the rest of the shift all taunted him with the obligatory 'five-finger shuffle' hand gesture.

It turned out that the stewardess hadn't reported the matter to the OIM at all; in fact, she was seen by Tommy leaving his office after having been in to empty the bin. The OIM did speak to her about the matter, but she just laughed it off. She'd worked on the rigs for a few years now, and she knew the level of shit he was going to get from the rest of the guys once the OIM had spoken to a few key people. No disciplinary action was required; Tommy's punishment was the level of utter embarrassment that he had to endure every time he went in the tea shack. A squad of scaffolders can have weeks of fun with that little beauty in their piss-taking armoury.

Tommy was renamed 'Tugger' for the rest of his time on the rig!

Inbetweenie

"I was on my Emergency Fire Team Member refresher course; we were in one of the smoke-filled modules in full BA sweating our tits off. It had been a long day of repeated exercises, and I was getting pretty pissed off now and ready for home. Through the smoke I could see the light at the end of the corridor and recognised it as the exit point and the end of what had to be the last exercise. The trainer stopped me and the guys; we were carrying a dummy casualty on a stretcher and our arms were hanging off. He pulled a piece of chalk from his pocket and drew a large circle on the deck and said 'There's a big hole in the deck there with a 30-metre drop to sea. What are you going to do?' There was a pause, and again he gestured 'Well, what's your plan?'

I snatched the piece of chalk out of his hands and drew two parallel lines across the hole and pointed at it shouting,

'That's a plank of fucking wood. Follow me, lads!' as I made my way across the imaginary bridge and into the cool fresh air."

CHAPTER 7

Health and Safety

The health and safety culture in the oil and gas industry and offshore is held in high regard by other industries who use it as a benchmark for their own safety practices. The work activities offshore along with the environment can be extremely hazardous, and over the years harsh lessons have been learnt at the tragic expense of those who have paid the ultimate price. Legislation, regulations, safe working practices and procedures have been implemented and fine-tuned to minimise the risk to personnel and equipment.

Each platform would have a health and safety advisor who oversees the health, safety and environmental working practices of the asset. There are various systems and campaigns to try to minimise the number of accidents and incidents and maintain the number of hours since the last recordable incident for as long as possible.

One such method is the safety card, an active monitoring safety system that has various names and versions depending on the company. The general theme is that members of the workforce are looking out for each other and stopping anyone from doing something that they deem to be unsafe. A conversation is held between workmates where they might point out a safer alternative way of working, or they could have identified a piece of equipment that could fail or cause harm if left unattended. Details of the conversation or the actions taken are recorded on the card and the learnings shared with the rest of the workforce. In theory, it's a no-blame culture where those in breach of safety remain anonymous and everyone learns from the mistakes whilst the safety system continues to evolve and improve day by day.

Teatime Teaser

Toolpusher briefing the team at the start of a large derrick overhaul project: "Gents, safety first on this project, you all know the reporting system for good and bad observations, we want to learn from all accidents, incidents and near misses and share good practices being used by all. Now go to work and be safe on my drill floor!"

One week later the Toolpusher was wearing a fall-arrest harness attached to steelwork just below the crown at the very top of the derrick. He was standing, straddling an open drop to the drill floor some 100 feet below. A series of events rapidly unfolded and some rigging failed, his safety line was snagged, and he was hurled up into the air and slammed back down onto the steelwork supports landing on his hands and knees like a petrified cat!

His first words to those who witnessed his acrobatics:

Toolpusher: "Not a fucking word of this to anyone! Understood?"

Tommy's Tale

It was another Baltic day offshore, and the wind was coming in hard from the Arctic north. The wind speeds weren't enough to put a stop to scaffolding, but they did cut through you like a knife as the wind chill had the effect of still air temperatures well into the minus numbers.

Tommy left the tea shack and made his way to the worksite to erect a small hop-up scaffold to give the pipefitters safe access to a valve and avoid them having to work on step ladders. The area was exposed to the wind, so Tommy was wrapped up with his storm jacket on and balaclava, and his safety glasses filled the gap around his eyes. In addition, he was wearing the normal overalls and gloves with a few extra layers on for good measure.

He was making his way down the stairs from the main deck to the cellar deck when he heard a voice behind telling him to hold onto the handrail. Tommy must only have gone down three steps and had every intention of holding on, but it was too late. He turned at the bottom of the stairs to see a guy in company overalls with HSE in big letters on the front of his V-Gard helmet. Tommy was only on the rig for one trip, so he didn't really know the guy apart from his induction on his first day. He was duly reminded of the need to hold the handrail and told what could happen if he were to fall down the metal stairs. Things then escalated. The imaginary story went on to outline that Tommy could be off work on sick pay due to injuries and the financial implications of not being able to pay the bills. "Bloody hell," Tommy thought. "Go easy with the guilt trip, big man!"

The safety advisor headed off and added that the conversation would be recorded on a card. Tommy nodded and thanked Mr Health & Safety in the anticipated 'proactive' manner that would avoid any bollockings and made his way to his work site.

The safety cards are collected throughout the day, and key cards are picked out and shared with the rest of the workforce. The idea being that everyone learns from the mistakes of others, it also gives the opportunity for feedback and extra advice from the guys as to how things should be done. On a lot of platforms, the cards are read out and elaborated on at the morning meeting, but here they were displayed on the notice board by grouping each day's cards together with a bulldog clip so that anyone could flick through and read them, not that many people did. It was only ever really the accused that went to read them, to see what their colleagues had to say about their actions.

Later that night, Tommy was walking past the offices on

his way to the TV room when he spotted the cards on the wall reminding him that he'd probably feature on one of them. He was keen to see what the safety bod had written about him, so he thumbed through skim-reading each card until he spotted his moment of fame. On the bottom of the card a Post-it note had been attached with a message saying, 'If you have taken the time to read through these cards then report to the safety advisor with this note to claim your safety award'. Often platforms have safety incentives and awards such as gifts or vouchers. Tommy slipped the note into his pocket and banked it for the following morning.

The next day, Tommy headed down to the office and presented the safety advisor with the note. To Tommy's disbelief, the guy was over the moon that someone had gone out of their way off-shift to read through the day's safety cards.

Mr Health & Safety took some keys out of his pocket and opened the large steel cabinet in the office whilst explaining to Tommy that he had actually stopped the guy on the stairs and that it was one of his cards that Tommy had been reading. He told him why he had stopped him and the importance of following the stair safety policy. Tommy soon realised that the guy didn't even recognise him. He put that down to all the cold-weather clobber he was wearing at the time.

The doors to the safety prize cupboard were open, and Tommy was invited to take his pick of the goods. There were watches, pens and MP3 players, but he opted for a DVD player thinking it would be ideal for his daughter's bedroom.

Throughout all this, the safety bod was still chirping on about his intervention and starting to do Tommy's head in. Once he had the DVD player in hand and was about to head out of the office, he turned to the safety guy with a smug look on his face and said:

"I know all that, mate. I was the one on the stairs that you stopped, but I didn't think I'd win a prize for it!!"

Inbetweenie

"One of the OIMs offshore had made some comments about us medics being surplus to requirements. Thankfully, our working life as a medic, when evaluated by the amount of time we spend treating people, is a quiet one. We do, however, cover a multitude of other roles and responsibilities that keep us busy. The OIM in question started hinting that his platform could operate without a medic and that first aiders could easily cover the role, that is until he had water retention issues and as his medic I had offered to insert a catheter to alleviate the pressure build-up in his bladder. It's funny how his attitude soon changed when I was about to slide a tube up into his urinary tract.

'If you'd prefer, I could ask Frank the mechanic to do this. I believe he's first-aid trained?'"

CHAPTER 8

Survival Suits

The offshore survival suit or flight suit has come in many variants over the years. The main aim of the suit is to keep the wearer dry and insulated from the cold seawater when submerged and in a survival situation. The design is such that it is waterproof when submerged, neck and wrist seals are tight enough to maintain a waterproof seal yet not so tight as to restrict circulation. There are neoprene gloves in a small pocket on each of the sleeves and a neoprene hood in the left-leg pocket on the front of the thigh. The suit material is bright yellow with reflective patches making the wearer more visible in the sea and is manufactured from flame-retardant material, providing optimum protection against a fire. Although the suit has a thermal liner, most companies have an added clothing policy of two layers in the summer and three layers of clothing to be worn when flying in winter; one layer must always be long sleeved. With the average water temperatures in the North Sea averaging 17°C (63°F) in summer and 6°C (43°F) in the winter, then the survival suit is a key piece of equipment should the unthinkable happen.

Teatime Teaser

Old hand offshore worker lies in his bed fully covered by his quilt. He's got his survival suit tucked in and hidden next to him. He pokes one arm through the sleeve and hangs it out of the bed in full view. Young engineer on his first trip offshore enters the cabin:

10pm – Old hand: "I hear there is going to be an emergency muster drill. Sleep in your survival suit like me to save time and we'll be the first ones down. The manager will be well impressed with ya!"

He then slides his arm out of the sleeve, chuckles to himself and goes to sleep, as he hears the young lad zipping himself into the sealed suit.

3am – Young engineer's voice whimpers out in the dark cabin: "Hi mate, are you awake? It's just that I've been to see the nightshift steward and he doesn't think there's going to be a lifeboat drill. I just thought you'd like to know, so you can take your survival suit off."

Old hand chuckles to himself before going back to sleep.

Tommy's Tale

The medic popped into the TV lounge for a quick head count to double-check he had roughly the right number of guys that were booked to fly in that day. He went down the list calling out the names. Although you seldom see people late for this meeting as it's the start of the trip home, some guys somehow still manage to forget. He passed around a clipboard and asked everyone to sign to say they had attended the flight brief and to note down how many bags they were taking in and the total weight. Prior to him coming in they were all sitting watching the football highlights. Naturally, he had a few complaints thrown at him when he switched it off and tried to turn on the HDMI feed to connect the DVD player. He fumbled around for a few more minutes whilst under verbal fire from the room until Tommy was volunteered to step up and sort it out. Not because they knew Tommy could do it, more because he was the youngest in the room and, therefore, he was expected to be the most 'tech savvy'. Within 30 seconds, Tommy had taken the two remote controls and proved everyone right by getting the flight safety video playing on the big screen.

"Sit yourself down, pops," Tommy said as he laughed at the medic, who was now settled in at the back of the room. Today was also his day to escape for two weeks, and he was ready for it.

During the video, the medic spotted Tommy thumbing through his phone, so he told him to switch the mobile off and watch the screen adding "Ya never know, son. You might actually learn something."

There was a snigger in the room, and Tommy sank down into his chair. After the briefing, the medic quickly phoned the radio room for an update on the flight.

"Right, gents, the aircraft has lifted Aberdeen, due on our deck in 50 minutes. Can everyone be in heli-admin in 20 minutes ready to suit up, please."

With this, they all made their way down to their muster points and collected their survival suits before heading upstairs to the waiting area.

Tommy stepped into heli-admin, took a seat, slipped off his trainers and stepped into his survival suit, just opting to to put on the lower half for now. Once his trainers were on, he sat and chilled out, waiting for the word to suit up. The medic stepped into the room and pulled on his long-sleeve top, saving the suiting-up process until it was necessary. He didn't want to start sweating before he needed to. A few minutes later, and the Helicopter Landing Officer (HLO) stuck his head through the outer door, "Suit up gents!"

Within a minute, Tommy had slipped his head through the neoprene neck seal and was fully zipped up. He squatted down whilst at the same time holding the neck seal open to expel the excess air and took a seat. By this time, the medic was at the half suited-up stage, and Tommy watched as he somehow managed to put his arm through the neck seal, whilst simultaneously his head went into the left sleeve opening. This is the equivalent of being strapped down in a strait jacket whilst blindfolded, and for comedy effect you have a two-foot-long yellow trunk that was your sleeve now sticking out the top of your head. It's a difficult manoeuvre to pull off but absolutely hilarious to anyone fortunate enough to witness it.

After a short delay to ensure everyone had seen the stage show, Tommy and a couple of the guys stepped in, got to grips with the situation and wrestled the medic free. With his beet-root-red face, he looked like he'd been slapped around by them, rather than helped.

"Are you OK, pops?" said Tommy. "I can quickly bob that DVD back on for you if ya want? Ya never know, you might learn something!"

"Fuck off!"

Inbetweenie

"I'm sure you've seen it when someone has a sudden sleep twitch and their legs and arms suddenly flick out. Even better is witnessing when someone is trying to stay awake, but their head does one big 'slam dunk' nod as if their spine has suddenly been removed. Finally, there is the classic where a person is sleeping, then out of the blue from their mouth comes a crazed involuntary random noise.

I came off night shift once and was asked to stay up an

extra couple of hours to sit in on a manager's meeting offshore with head office patched in via video conferencing. To top it off, I had some 'big wig' from Houston sat at my table. The room was really warm and stuffy, and the lights were dimmed. All I wanted to do was sleep. The company man was stood up by a large screen just droning on as he presented his flow charts and statistics when without warning I was out cold, fast asleep. My head dropped, my legs lashed out and kicked the American guy sat opposite me as I uncontrollably shouted out some incoherent phrase, before falling backwards from my chair and onto the floor!

I was politely asked to leave the room."

CHAPTER 9

Drugs and Alcohol

The oil and gas industry has strict drugs and alcohol controls. Each duty holder and contracting company will enforce their own policy; however, overall, they are all intent on preventing the use or abuse of illegal or prohibited substances amongst offshore workers.

At any time from checking in for your flight to arriving back onshore you could be asked to attend a drugs or alcohol test either as part of a random test or due to the suspicion that there has been an abuse of the policy.

In general, those who fail the test will face disciplinary action by their employing company and will undoubtedly be flown off the platform for additional tests or counselling. Most companies offer help to employees who have a problem with substance abuse, and there are support procedures in place. Some companies have a policy that should an employee identify that they have a problem or require support prior to a test taking place, the company can arrange for a medical assessment, rehabilitation or a treatment programme. In general, and in the interest of everyone working offshore, there is zero tolerance towards employees or third parties who do not obey the drug and alcohol policy on the platform.

Teatime Teaser

Medic to drug test candidate: "I need you to go into that toilet and fill this cup with a sample to be tested, leave it on top of the toilet, wash your hands and step back outside."

5 minutes later – candidate looking bewildered: "It's all yours."

Medic: "You dirty bastard!!!"

He'd shit in the cup!

Tommy's Tale

It had been a strange day on the rig. One of the newly arrived guys had yesterday been pulled into the OIM's office, and in no time at all he was suited up and in heli-admin waiting on the next flight off. He had arranged to have drugs posted to the platform and had been challenged by the manager when he went to collect the package after appearing unsettled when he was enquiring about the next postal delivery, which raised a few suspicions and drew attention to himself. That was the last time he was seen on the rig, and no doubt the last time he worked in the North Sea.

Tommy and Steve were down in their cabin working through some reports. It was often the case that there was no office space and the only alternative was to disappear off to your room to work. Not ideal, Tommy thought, given you are cooped up in there all night, but on the flip side you could have the telly on quietly in the background, so not all bad.

They'd been in the cabin for just over an hour when Tommy offered to go and get a couple of teas and see what biscuits were on offer. As he headed past the gym, he casually glanced through the window to see some guy waving his arms around and nattering away as if doing some kind of exercise but certainly not dressed for it. Given some of the weirdos that can be seen on the rig, he didn't really dwell on it. He just smiled to himself and kept on walking.

He headed to the tea point in the rec (recreation) room and made two teas, capped them off with plastic lids and made his way back towards the cabin. Just as he went to pass the gym, the door opened and out bounded a dog on a lead closely followed by its master.

"What the Fu...," Tommy said. "Dog..." He couldn't even string his words together; the sight of a dog offshore had completely messed with his head. The spaniel was bounding all over the place with its tail going like the clappers. The dog was probably the happiest of any of them on board, Tommy thought as he watched it doing the wall of death around the rec room as it went about its work. The safety advisor who was with them explained to Tommy that it was a follow-up action from the recent drug incident, and as such a sniffer dog had been brought out to check the accommodation. He also pointed out that the dog would be searching all the cabins soon and asked him to step outside when he heard them knock at the door.

Tommy headed back to the cabin, but en route thought there's no way he was going to tell his mate; he wanted to see the look on his face when the K9 missile came through the door. He got back to the cabin and handed over the tea, getting no thanks at all, only to be asked "Where's the biscuits?" Tommy didn't tell him that he got a little distracted.

Steve put his cup of tea to one side, declared he was going to 'drop the kids off at the pool' and stepped into the toilet. Normally this would be the cue for your roommate to leave the cabin, but Tommy didn't want to miss the show. He also noted that Steve hadn't locked the toilet door… Priceless!

Tommy could hear the dog approaching the cabin, so he stood up and went to the door to save any knocks that would warn of the four-legged maniac that was about to pay them a visit. The dog handler recognised Tommy from earlier and asked if it was OK to go in. He instantly opened the toilet door; the dog leapt in to be met by the weirdest scream and commotion. The spaniel bolted out, Steve leapt up with piss running down his legs and the magazine he was reading went flying. Tommy was absolutely creased up laughing and couldn't control himself to apologise to the safety advisor or the dog handler, who were both themselves still in shock. No further drugs were found, and Steve's cup of tea went cold whilst he showered and changed.

Later that day, Steve had the last laugh as Tommy went down in the history books for being the only person to stand in dog shit whilst working on a North Sea platform.

Inbetweenie

"Our afternoon flight offshore was cancelled, and we were scheduled onto a flight the following morning. There were three of us heading to the platform for the first time, but we'd worked together on other jobs. Once clear of the heliport, we hopped in a taxi along with another older and somewhat dishevelled-looking guy from our flight. We dropped him at a lounge bar in town. He said he lived locally but would call for a quick pint before going home. The rest of us headed to our hotel and out for something to eat, a couple of beers and a catch-up. When you are having a laugh, it's hard to stop drinking after a couple of pints, but we valued our jobs more and it just wasn't worth the risk.

Early the next morning, we arrived at the heliport and checked in for the flight. In no time at all, we were suited up and making our way out to the helicopter. The pre-flight safety briefing was in quite a small room, and it soon became apparent that someone hadn't stopped drinking early. The room smelt like a brewery! The general opinion, although nobody actually vocalised it, was that it was the old dishevelled-looking guy sat in the back corner, whom we had dropped off at the bar the evening before. Only now he looked even worse for wear! On the flight, I was sat next to him and it was clear that this was the guy who had slipped through the net and was lucky to have made it out to work. Even the extra-strong mints that he kept chomping on weren't doing anything to disguise the smell.

We arrived on the platform and were told to get our paperwork sorted out and check off our equipment. The following morning, we were to meet the OIM for the usual green-hat talk before being set free on the platform to start work. The three of us made our way down to his office. I knocked on the door and heard the request, 'Come in, guys, and grab a seat. I won't keep you long but as with all offshore installations it's safety first!'

The OIM was a very smart-looking, yet once dishevelled, older-looking guy."

CHAPTER 10

Offshore Helicopter Operations

By the end of 2015, the fleet of helicopters operating in the United Kingdom Continental Shelf (UKCS) totalled 86 aircraft. This consisted of 24 medium-class helicopters and 62 heavy class; a number of aircraft had been removed from service following a recent downturn within the industry and less demand for airframes. During 2015, the fleet flew over 69,000 hours with over 825,000 passengers, a significant reduction from the previous year when over 1.5 million passengers were transported.

From 1996 to the end of 2015, there had been four fatal accidents resulting in the tragic loss of lives of 38 offshore workers and helicopter crew. Two of these accidents were attributed to catastrophic component failure and two associated with human factors. In addition, there had also been 16 non-fatal accidents during the same period.

A 2015 report by Oil & Gas UK quotes the accident rate for a fatal accident over the previous five-year period was on or below 0.6 per 100,000 flying hours.

Teatime Teaser

On an in-field helicopter flight from a main complex platform to a Normally Unmanned Installation (NUI).

Passenger (tapping pilot on the shoulder): "I think we are going the wrong way, mate." He points out of the window to his left. "I think we need to be going that way!"

Pilot (pointing at his Electronic Navigation System): "On the contrary, we are on course for XX and will be there in five mins."

Passenger: "That's great, but we are meant to be going to YY today!"

The red-faced pilots bank the aircraft around to the left.

Tommy's Tale

Suited up and sitting in heli-admin is always a good feeling. Tommy was ready for the off along with the rest of his crew, who all had that 'best job in the world' feeling. The noise of the aircraft hovering over the deck as it slowly touched its wheels down had been long awaited. The aircraft's engines slowed to a quieter throb as the oncoming crew disembarked and made their way down the stairs to heli admin. Most of the oncoming crew had back-to-backs who were waiting to grab their lifejackets and give a quick condensed handover detailing the activities of the last two weeks in 30 seconds. Most of the time, the oncoming crew have been up since stupid o'clock, then waited around the heliport for a good couple of hours before being crammed into a helicopter. Tired and suitably depressed, the verbal handover just washes over them as they give their life jacket to the more enthusiastic of the two, who is heading home. Tommy was one of those about to go home, and he knew there was no point telling his back-to-back anything constructive, so he just had a quick catch-up and told him the written handover was on the desk.

After the helicopter had been refuelled, the HDA signalled for the guys to follow him up to the helideck. The medic had checked all of the guys' lifejackets and EBA bottles for the minimum required 200 bar, all survival suit zips were fully fastened and sealed, and they were good to go. Tommy dropped to the back of the line, knowing this would mean he got one of the door seats with better leg room for the flight in; being tall he needed all he could get.

Two of the guys in front of him instantly took the piss. "If you are scared to fly just say!" they said, intimating that Tommy was more interested in the emergency exit than the additional leg room.

The two guys laughed with each other. Tommy overheard the other comment, "I don't understand why people don't admit to a fear of flying. They should have to wear a pink armband!"

It was all water off a duck's back to Tommy; he'd done

plenty of hours in the air over the years and had nothing to prove. He also didn't blame anyone for wanting to sit next to an escape window. There aren't many guys who would happily sit with someone between them and an emergency exit if they didn't have to.

They boarded the aircraft, and Tommy had again managed to get the seat by the door. The HLO checked everyone's harnesses were fastened and adjusted one of the guy's straps so they weren't covering his lifejacket. The door was closed, the HLO left the helideck and after a quick visual check he gave the pilots the thumbs-up.

The aircraft slowly lifted, hovered for a second and once it had turned slightly into wind it pulled away from the platform. The flight in was a little bumpy due to a headwind but after a few power naps they were soon approaching Aberdeen Airport. The pilots lined up the aircraft with the runway and gave the normal spiel about having a safe trip onshore and we look forward to seeing you again soon, to which as a passenger you're thinking "Thanks very much… and not too soon, pal, eh? I'm not even home yet!"

On final approach, the pilots could be seen fiddling with the switches on the console, and the aircraft flared and went into a hover rather than the expected roll out down the runway. The pilot came over the intercom to state that they had an indication that the landing gear wasn't down and they were awaiting instruction. Tommy could see the fire tenders with flashing lights pulling out of the station and heading towards them. One of the guys who had earlier been taunting Tommy was frantically looking around and appearing a little anxious. The next update from the captain was that they were going to fly across the airfield nearer to the tower where they were going to try and get a visual of the landing gear. The fire engines were tracking their every move, which unsettled Tommy's mate even more.

The captain soon gave another update explaining that things were still inconclusive and that an engineer would be coming out to take a closer look. Sure enough, in no time at all a guy was standing in his fluorescent jacket looking up at the gear as the pilot held the aircraft in a perfect hover overhead.

Tommy couldn't resist it and told the two piss-takers "If the gear won't go down, we'll have to jump out onto the grass one at a time."

"Ya fuckin what?!?!" said the weaker of the two, now drip white and sweating.

After a few more minutes hovering, the captain confirmed they had the all-clear and tracked across to an area of tarmac to land and taxi over to the stand to disembark. Shortly after the flight, they were all taken into a briefing room where the situation was explained, and any questions answered. It was likely to be a false indication or faulty sensor, but the aircraft would be taken out of service whilst it was fully checked over and the issue resolved.

Once debriefed, they all headed out of the door for home,

but Tommy couldn't resist turning to Mr Pink Armband and saying…

"If you're scared to fly mate, just say!"

Inbetweenie

"I was part of a three-man team and we'd arrived on the small platform for a one-off job. It had a very family feel about it (almost inbred) although we weren't exactly made to feel part of the family. Maybe when there's no outsiders there they all liked to walk about naked at night and we'd come on board and spoilt it for them.

The three of us on the team made our way into the galley at dinner time and found ourselves towards the front of the queue. Our TL was a mountain of a man with hands like shovels and clearly as hard as nails, but he had a level of wit that could shoot anyone down along with the confidence to use it.

We grabbed some food and chose a table to sit at. I noticed a couple of guys in the queue gesture towards us, and then one of them came to our table arrogantly stating 'We've sat in those seats for the last 10 years, pal.'

In an instant, the big man reached down to the foot of his chair, grabbed the base of one of the legs and extended the chair out in front of him with one arm as an offering. 'Sorry, mate, I didn't see any brass plaques on them. It's all yours,' he said with a straight tone and a don't-fuck-with-me stare. Looking stunned, the guy took the chair and our man just grabbed another from the next table, winked at me and sat down in exactly the same spot that had been contested.

The entire galley went quiet. We still didn't feel like part of the family, but from that point on we weren't told where we could and couldn't sit."

CHAPTER 11

Offshore Installations/Platforms

There are various types of offshore installations and platforms that are in service around the globe. The environment and operational requirements will dictate the type used on any given project. The shallow waters of the North Sea are more suited to fixed installations, jack-up platforms or less common compliant tower structures. In the case of fixed platforms, the jacket (structural frame/legs) is floated into position on a barge and either tipped into the sea or lowered via a heavy lifting crane. Piles are driven into the sea floor to secure the jacket that forms the support for the topside decks and facilities, which are lifted on in modular form. Such installations can comprise of multiple jackets with interconnecting bridges. These jackets will all support different services such as drilling, production, compression and living quarters. For deeper waters such as the Gulf of Mexico, floating platforms are used like that of the Perdido, which is a spar platform in a water depth of 2,450 metres (8,040 ft).

Teatime Teaser

Early 80s telephone conversation between head office and offshore construction:

Senior management onshore: "We are sending out a safety officer to ensure things run smoothly and incident free."

Construction superintendent: "Absolute waste of time and a waste of a useful offshore bed!"

The onshore management team ignore the antiquated comments made by the superintendent, recruit a safety consultant and mobilise him to go offshore. A week later, the construction superintendent receives word that there is a safety officer on the outbound flight, due to arrive on the platform in the next 30 minutes.

Telephone conversation between construction superintendent and the platform radio room:

Construction superintendent: "Find out the name of the safety officer on this next flight and book him a seat straight back in again. He ain't stayin' on this rig!"

The aircraft lands, and the superintendent identifies the safety officer.

Construction superintendent: "You can keep your survival suit on, young man. You're going straight back where you came from, pal. Have a safe trip home."

…How times have changed!

Tommy's Tale

It was the early 1980s and a long time coming, but finally the platform was ready for first gas following a long hook-up and commissioning programme. Tommy was one of the first batch of operators to work on the platform and was due to fly off-shore later that day. He had been asked to meet some company men at the heliport prior to boarding the flight for what was quite a unique request.

A local man had recently passed away; he had served his time at sea with the nearby fishing fleet. Keen to support the local communities, the oil company had agreed to scatter his ashes over the southern North Sea from one of the routine flights to the platform.

"A fitting final resting place," Tommy thought. "But why me?"

It had been agreed that the guy nearest the door would slide it open just enough for the canister with the ashes to be poked through the gap and the passing airstream would draw out the ashes from the open top. Once empty, the canister would stay in the helicopter, the door closed, and they would simply carry on with the flight.

En route, the guy by the door started to over-think things; so too did Tommy. He cracked the seal of the canister open in his hand and twisted the top a quarter of a thread and then closed it again. He didn't want to be like his wife at home, un-able to open a jam jar and end up passing it around the other passengers for assistance. The guy by the door had been briefed by the crew on how to partly slide it open, but he too could be seen staring at the handle intently going through the simple steps in his mind. After all, there's something not quite right about opening the door of a helicopter that's at 2,000 feet. In turn, curiosity got the better of him, and although a little early he thought it best to open the door very slightly until the locks disengaged. Then when the time was right all he had to do was slide it open. Unknown to him, Tommy had also given in to curiosity, and he wanted to see the contents of his 'carry-on luggage'. He opened the jar at the exact time that the door seal was broken, and a blast of air rushed over the top of the open canister whilst Tommy was peering inside. The rapid gush of air created a Venturi effect and threw up a dust cloud into the cabin, coating everyone in the deceased's ashes, including the pilots. Tommy thought quick on his feet, was able to get the canister to the door and just hurled it out. The 2,000-foot drop would surely be enough to scatter the remaining contents. The door was quickly closed and everyone sat stunned for the rest of the flight. No more stunned than the helideck crew on the platform when they saw the dusty, powder-coated passengers that stepped off the aircraft, quite literally with ashen faces and dusty white hair.

HLO: "Jeez, you lot look like you've seen a ghost!"

Inbetweenie

"It had been a long flight with an extended route due to the bad weather that came in blocking our path. I should have gone to the loo before we suited up but thought I'd be OK. We were diverted to fly to another platform, and whilst there the aircraft took on some fuel. We waited in a safe area and had to stay suited up as it was only for around five minutes. It was outside and I was absolutely freezing, not a good thing when you're bursting for a pee. Once fuelled, we hopped back on and headed to the rig. By this time my bladder felt like a football and it was all getting a bit desperate. When we landed, we stepped off the helicopter and were immediately met by the safety advisor, who said it was late and he would give us a very quick internal accommodation induction, with the full external guided tour in the morning.

'Keep your survival suits on and follow me. It won't take long,' he said and off he trooped.

To this day I don't know what came over me. It's like my bladder heard the guy and just thought 'Ah, fuck it!' and opened the flood gates!

I did a 10-minute induction with a pint of piss in each survival suit leg, but at least my feet were warm."

CHAPTER 12

North Sea Oil and Gas Sectors

Five countries have stakes in the production of oil and gas in the North Sea: the United Kingdom, Norway, Denmark, Holland and the smallest being Germany. The respective sectors are divided by median lines as decided in the late 1960s; however, oil was commercially recovered much earlier than this.

For the UK sector, personnel are flown offshore from four key locations, Scatsta in the Shetlands; Dyce, which is five miles north of Aberdeen; Humberside; and Norwich. Both Norwich and Humberside heliports service the southern North Sea. All heliports have flight links with Aberdeen. Passengers for Scatsta check in via Aberdeen to be flown north by fixed-wing aircraft for their connecting helicopter flight offshore.

To work in the UK Oil and Gas sector, workers are required to attend and pass a Basic Offshore Safety Induction and Emergency Training (BOSIET) course.

The course forms part of a common offshore safety induction process which provides an awareness of the hazards encountered when travelling to and from offshore installations, as well as an introduction to the offshore safety regime and safety management systems. There is also theoretical and practical training in sea survival as well as first aid, basic firefighting and helicopter safety and escape training. In addition, candidates have the option to attend further training which covers all of the requirements under the agreement for mutual recognition which is recognised by the UK, Norway, Netherlands and Denmark, allowing them to work in the additional sectors.

Teatime Teaser

On his first overseas offshore trip, the young english safety engineer had been told he could find Jeroen, the Dutch safety officer, on the helideck during lunch break. He thought it best to don full PPE (Personal Protective Equipment), so he arrived on the helideck in hard hat, overalls, gloves, safety glasses and rig boots, first impressions and all that!

Dutch safety officer: "Thanksh for coming, although you're a little overdreshed my friend, but ya OK. I just thought I'd take the opportunity to introdoosh myshelf before this afternoon's management meeting."

The Dutch safety officer stood up to shake hands with his new replacement; in contrast he was wearing a black thong, gold framed sunglasses and a gallon of coconut sun lotion.

First impressions well and truly made.

Tommy's Tale

The maintenance team had flown the short hop from the main complex (manned platform) to the Normally Unmanned Installation (NUI) for a day of planned work. It was only a stone's throw away as far as flying was concerned, but as far as Tommy was aware it was the only option open to them. They had a communications engineer with them as well that day, who really didn't want to be there as it would only take two minutes for him to reset the fault and he had more pressing work to finish back on the main complex. "Tough!" Tommy thought. "Welcome to my world. You're stuck for the day."

Once they had taken off their survival suits from the flight, they started the day with fresh coffee, none of the cheap instant sludge that you get back in the UK sector. One of the guys had even brought some pastries that had been baked the previous night. It was a leisurely start preparing permits and paperwork, before getting on with the jobs in hand, but it was the way of working that Tommy had become accustomed to since starting his new job in the Danish sector.

Tommy made his way down onto the cellar deck to inspect some of the safety equipment for recertification. Whilst there, he heard a strange noise coming from the direction of the main complex. The noise got gradually louder: 'put-put-put-put-put-put'. It was the sound of a diesel inboard engine, and Tommy could see what appeared to be a lifeboat slowly coming into view. The main complex had a spare one on davits that could be used for close standby cover when needed, not quite the Fast Rescue Craft (FRC) that Tommy had been accustomed to offshore, but regardless there was no over-the-side work today, so he wondered what they were doing here. The next thing Tommy knew, the comms engineer was coming down the stairs with his survival suit on shouting "OK, Tommy, that's me finished for the day. See you later!" With that he climbed down the escape-to-sea ladder and threw himself into the sea.

"What the fuck!" Tommy thought as he watched the guys on the lifeboat scoop him into the door at the stern. Then the boat turned and made its way back to the main platform. No sooner had Tommy got over the shock of that than the noise of the engines started to get louder again, and he noticed that the boat had made a U-turn and was heading back in their direction. This time, however, there was a plume of smoke coming from it. It turned out they'd had a small engine fire, all the more evident as the comms engineer had thrown himself back into the water and climbed back on board the platform via the escape to sea ladder. In fact, one of the other guys did the same. The 'captain of the ship' steered it away from the NUI to a safe location where the standby vessel took it in tow.

The comms engineer said, "The water is cold, Tommy, but there is a nice fire on the lifeboat to keep you toasty, my friend!"

Tommy replied, "It's OK mate, I'll fly back, but thanks for the offer."

The lifeboat sank later that day!

Inbetweenie

"We were flying to the platform daily due to lack of beds off-shore. I asked one of the guys to tidy the back of my hair with his electric trimmer. My hair was slightly styled at the front or at least tidy, and I just wanted the back squaring up to save a trip to the barber's. With one guy manning the clippers and another egging him on, the razor guard was flicked off and before I could stop the assault, a chunk of hair down to my scalp had been removed from my fringe right back to the middle of my head. I was mortified, and the more pissed off I got, the more the two of them just stood there laughing. As I looked at my new centre parting that was as wide as a motorway, I realised the only option I had was to let them finish the job and completely remove all the hair from my head taking me down to the bone. It had been a red-hot summer and my tanned face was now topped off with a milky white dome. For the next week or so, everywhere I went people just stared, the worst being when I was offshore in the smoke room and the platform manager sat opposite me. I could just feel his eyes burning into me as he scrutinised my two-tone head. I glanced up as he was leaving; he simply shook his head and walked out.

By the next trip, I had grown a full beard, so too had a few of the guys on the team. We were pretty much split 50/50 Scottish/English, and a conversation started on how much us 'jocks' apparently swear all of the time. Obviously, we denied such claims, and it was decided that the only way to resolve the dispute was via a bet. Whoever swore first had to shave half of their beard off, straight down the middle. One side of your face had to be clean shaven, the other still sporting a beard. In addition, if challenged, you weren't allowed to discuss or comment on the reason why this had been done. You just had to walk around looking like a cock for the next 24 hours. The challenge had begun, and within five minutes I'd dropped my guard and declared how 'shit' something was, followed shortly after by taunts from the English amongst us that I had to go and have half a shave as promised.

The following day, I was sat in the same smoke room with the same manager sat opposite me and yet again I could sense his stare from across the room. Depending on which profile view of my face that you had, it either looked like I had a full beard, or I was clean shaven. He, however, had a square-on, frontal view and could therefore see both versions.

He shook his head. 'Humour me, what the fuck is wrong with you?'

As per the bet, I couldn't say anything."

CHAPTER 13

The Helideck

The helideck consists of a large green surface area, or in the case of aluminium decks, this can be left as metal grey due to the difficulties of coating the material. All landing areas must be finished with a non-slip surface/coating. There are several mandatory markings on the deck including the landing circle or Touchdown Positioning Marking (TD/PM circle) which is painted yellow. In the centre of the circle there is a white heliport identification marking 'H'. This is aligned with a black chevron towards one edge of the helideck which indicates the landing area (and D-circle) and extends over a sector of at least 210°. The purpose of the chevron is to provide visual guidance to the HLO so that he can ensure that the 210° is clear of obstructions before giving a helicopter clearance to land. Around the perimeter of the helideck there are large stencilled numbers (D values) which signify the largest dimension of a helicopter when the rotors are turning that can land within the circle.

The Helicopter Landing Officer (HLO) and any Helideck Assistants (HDAs) using VHF aeronautical radio equipment are required to hold a UK CAA Offshore Aeronautical Radio Station Operator's Certificate of Competence. On approach the pilot must request deck availability from the HLO or platform radio operator (RO) prior to landing. The radios will also be used for any requests, such as a refuel or queries either on approach or when on deck, as well as critical communications in an emergency.

The helideck is equipped with various forms of firefighting and emergency response equipment. Helideck emergency teams have the capability to apply foam via a fixed monitor or hoses primarily to extinguish aviation fuel fires. They also have dry powder, CO_2 and water media available for additional classes of fire. All areas of the helideck including all of the systems, procedures and competencies are frequently inspected and audited to ensure each platform is compliant with legislation as governed by the Central Aviation Authority.

Teatime Teaser

Aircraft on deck, rotors turning, and passengers are all loaded ready for their flight home when the pilot's radio crackles into life as he speaks to the HLO.

Pilot: "HLO, the wind has dropped considerably, and looking at our revised routing we're going to have to bump 120kgs… sorry, mate!"

HLO: "OK, that'll be two passengers then, wait one and we'll remove two guys and sort the manifest."

Pilot (turning to look at the passengers seated behind him):
"You could just remove the big salad dodger from the middle row, he should cover it!"

Tommy's Tale

The platform was an old asset, run down and rusty, made worse by the stench of seagull shit that was baked onto everything. The satellite (NUI) was due to be shut down and decommissioned. Over the next few days they would be visiting there to carry out some essential maintenance and safety checks prior to a jack-up platform coming alongside to perform final decommissioning. When the aircraft landed, the pilot warned the HLO that he would be submitting a report regarding the obscured helideck markings and that the guano (bird shit) would need to be cleaned off if they wanted to return the next day.

As there was a jet-wash unit on board, two of the guys were given the thankless task of spending the day blasting the deck with sea water which was being drawn up by a small lift pump lowered over the side. The resulting fish sludge soup was then washed off the deck into the drains and away to sea. Tommy was there to carry out safety checks, and much to the other guys' dislike he managed to escape getting involved in the jet-washing job.

The platform didn't have the best of facilities either as the toilet was also out of order. During the morning toolbox talk, the OIM explained that everyone would have to pee over the side as the toilet was out of bounds. Tommy hinted that he might need more than a pee and wondered what the contingency plan was. The manager told him to show some restraint and hold it in for the day, but after last night's curry Tommy couldn't promise anything.

The OIM pointed out "It's one thing peeing over the side, but you're not poking your arse through the handrail for a shite. I'm not having you falling overboard backwards. I wouldn't want to explain why you were rescued from the sea with you pants down!"

The day had progressed well, and the helideck was looking pretty good. Tommy had also just about finished his work, and they were all having an extended afternoon tea break. Tommy, who had been complaining all day that he needed a dump, decided enough was enough and he simply had to go. The OIM insisted that he hold it in, but whilst everyone was downstairs Tommy decided he would quickly go onto the helideck and use a plastic bag to catch the contents. He tucked the bag in his pocket and made his way onto the helideck.

There are two access stairs to the helideck which can be used to board the helicopter from either side, depending which way the pilot lands due to the wind direction. Tommy was just in the final strains of his 'unloading' and facing one set of stairs not knowing that the OIM was coming up the stairs to his 'rear' along with the helideck jet washing team. The OIM wanted to see for himself how clean it was, and the lads were keen to show off the results of their hard work. Tommy was just about finished and about to stand up as the manager and his proud team stepped onto the deck behind him.

OIM: "What the fuck are doing? Oh, I need to hear your explanation to these two as to why you've just shit on their parade!"

Inbetweenie

"I had been on a course during my leave when I was younger. I didn't have a car, so I travelled to Aberdeen via train. I was going to claim the price of the rail fare back on expenses when a mate of mine pointed out that I would make more money if I claimed the mileage. I ran the numbers in my head and opted for the imaginary car that would give me an extra £30 return.

I don't know why but on my way offshore I noted down a random registration plate from the carpark for my expense sheet and wrote down the first cheap model of car I could think of. It was one that my boss would see as within my budget and seal the deal to my extra £30. I completed the paperwork and handed it in for approval. Shortly after submitting it, my manager asked to see me. When I went into his office, he had my expense form on the desk in front of him.

'So how do you like the Ford Fiesta?' he asked.

'Not bad,' I said. 'I'm saving for something better though.'

'Yeah, I love my new BM. You won't have seen it though

as I'm in the wife's car this trip. But you've clearly seen that, or at least the fucking number plates according to your expenses!'

I didn't get my £30, or my rail fare, or keep my job."

CHAPTER 14

Liferafts

The primary means of escape from any offshore platform would always be via helicopter, given the speed by which personnel can be evacuated to safety. Depending on the nature of the emergency, helicopters may not be available or deemed a safe option, and therefore alternative methods of escape to sea will always be added to the safety case. These could include davit and freefall launched lifeboats, escape-to-sea lowering systems (a single-person harness), evacuation chute systems (essentially a netted zigzag slide that deploys with liferafts at the base) or the common liferaft that is tipped from a cradle from the platform; once in the water, a lanyard is pulled which activates the CO_2 cartridges for rapid inflation.

Liferafts come in various designs, the most common of which is the 'throw overboard' liferaft which can cater for varying numbers of personnel depending on the model, such as 16, 20, 25 or 35-man liferafts.

The liferaft is stored within a toughened resin container

on one of the lowest process decks of the platform. This would typically be around 20 metres above sea level, where they are protected from wave damage in high seas. The liferaft containers are mounted on cradles, which allows them to be easily deployed into the sea. The container will then float on the surface and remain attached to the platform via a rope. Personnel would descend ladders from the level where the liferaft was deployed (generally the cellar deck) and climb down to the spider deck, usually around six metres above sea level. From here they can access a line to activate the CO_2 cylinders and inflate the liferaft.

The line is left attached to the platform, allowing personnel to pull the liferaft into location at the base of an escape-to-sea ladder where it can then be boarded. Once all personnel are on board, the line is cut and the liferaft can then drift free from the platform.

The liferafts have a pull-up roof to shelter the personnel on board from the elements as well as containing an emergency pack with equipment such as flares, a first aid kit and a locator beacon. There will also be a sea anchor, similar to a small parachute that is deployed into the water and attached via a line. The sea anchor stabilises the liferaft in rough seas and prevents it from uncontrollably spinning during helicopter-winching operations should the occupants be lifted to safety via a rescue helicopter.

Teatime Teaser

It was a number of years ago, and we were doing our offshore survival training. This included some liferaft simulation exercises in the harbour area, just off the quayside. For one of the drills, we had to ensure the liferaft was secure for rough sea conditions. This meant raising the side panels and fastening them above our heads to form a roof. With eight of us seated in the sealed raft, things soon became very hot and humid. A line was then attached to the raft, and we were spun around by the instructor, who was driving a boat with an outboard engine. This was to simulate rough sea conditions and the importance of deploying the sea anchor. We'd failed to do this when we boarded the liferaft, and the instructor was about to make us pay for our oversight. It clearly worked, as one of the guys threw up everywhere. The combination of the fast-rotating liferaft and projectile vomiting ensured we were all covered in the tangy, salty puke!

By the time the side panels were dropped, there had been a knock-on effect from the smell which escalated the situation. The instructor was greeted by eight guys all covered in vomit which was now swilling around us all as we sat in a pool of stench!

We opted to go against all of the pre-discussed survival training and threw ourselves into the sea.

Tommy's Tale

Tommy fancied a change of scene from the mundane routine maintenance that he had been tasked with over the last week, so when the opportunity came to install a new liferaft on the cellar deck, he jumped at the chance. He'd never actually installed a liferaft before, but he knew the apprentice that would be helping him had recently installed one on the previous trip, so he just blagged his way onto the job by saying he'd done it all before and knew exactly what to do.

Tommy and his young helper lifted the liferaft onto the cradle and secured it in position, at which point there was a tannoy for the apprentice asking him to call the control room. The young lad took the call on a nearby phone, and then returned to the job only to explain to Tommy that he had been called to help one of the operators with some isolations and that a replacement pair of hands would be sent over to assist Tommy shortly.

Thankfully, nobody had realised that it was Tommy who was assisting the apprentice rather than the other way around. The young lad had vanished before Tommy had the chance to grill him on how to finish the job. Not long after he had gone, Tommy was joined by the new apprentice, who had only been offshore a few trips and had only seen a liferaft on his survival course, so he didn't know much about them, let alone how to install one.

Tommy knew his work would be inspected by the safety

technician prior to the liferaft being classed as in service, but he also knew that if he cocked it up he'd be the brunt of a few jokes in the tea shack. With that, he opted to swallow his pride and phone the safety tech for some much-needed instruction with regard to tying off the painter line and ensuring it would deploy to sea without inflating in midair. Whilst he went to the phone, Tommy instructed the new lad to coil up the old line from the previous liferaft and tidy things up prior to the safety tech coming to pay them a visit, which was the result Tommy wanted.

Tommy was only a few metres away on the phone and had managed to convince the tech to come down and check his work, which was nearly complete. Even better, the tech had agreed to come and help him finish the job off. What a result! Just as Tommy went to put the phone down, there was a loud popping sound behind him, and he turned to see a stunned-looking apprentice holding the wrong piece of rope in his hand and a huge orange monster rapidly trying to manifest itself into a liferaft behind him. In sheer panic, and to this day he doesn't know why, Tommy ran and dived onto the liferaft in some vain hope of preventing it from fully inflating. Instead it swallowed him up and then flipped him into the air pinning him upside down against a diagonal steel support. Not long after that, the safety tech arrived on site to see Tommy pinned in position, upside down, frantically shouting at the apprentice to pull him out! The safety tech located the purge valves, and slowly the orange monster withered away, allowing Tommy to slump to the floor, which is where he was laid trying to come to terms with things as the safety tech rightly pointed out,

"I guess you'll be requesting another liferaft, then?"

Inbetweenie

"During a scaffolding job over the side of the platform, I was the standby man with the radio. I was supervising the guys working at height above the sea whilst being the radio link between the worksite and the standby vessel in the event of an emergency.

It had been a long morning, and I was finding it all tedious, that is, until a seal popped up on the surface and was looking up at the guys on the job. With my best seal impression, I called out to it, and to my amazement it called back. I got the attention of the lads on the scaffold, and they could see the seal below them.

'Watch this!' I shouted and again I let out my best seal impression, but this time it just ignored me. The lads laughed and hurled a bit of abuse but went quiet when I let out another call, this time longer and louder, and I added some seal flipper claps. Again, it just sat there in the water but again didn't have the decency to return my call.

'Be like that then, ya miserable fucker!' I said, thinking out loud, when a voice piped up behind me, 'Say please next time, son.' I turned to see the platform OIM, platform safety advisor and Operations Team Leader stood just a few feet behind me.

That night, I went into the galley for my meal only to be greeted by a chorus of seal calls, and the chef handed me a plate with a single fresh mackerel on it.

Followed by 'When you've eaten that you can show us all how you can balance a ball on your nose!'"

CHAPTER 15

Emergency Shutdown

Offshore oil and gas platforms have a wide range of safety systems on board to both monitor and make the installation safe in the event of an emergency. These range from automated or manually activated systems and devices including Emergency Shutdown (ESD) systems, fire and gas (F&G) detection systems, Manual Alarm Call Points (MACPs) and communications systems.

Following the Piper Alpha disaster and the Cullen report, the UK offshore sector invested heavily in the safety of offshore platforms, one specific area being the automated and manual safety systems. The Health and Safety Executive (HSE) also increased its numbers of inspectors who specialised in the offshore oil and gas industry.

Oil and gas production figures are monitored closely on a shift-by-shift basis. However, the workforce is made fully aware that safety must come first in the event of a loss of containment of any hydrocarbons, either from a safety aspect or one of protecting the environment. As such, all work parties on site ensure that they are aware of the safety systems that are local to where they are working or that can be found on their escape route or when heading to the muster point in the event of an emergency. Prior to work commencing, the work party leader would identify and brief the team on the location of the nearest telephone and emergency number, MAC point and ESD button, as well as ensuring the team are aware of the escape route options and any other safety resources or procedures that apply.

Teatime Teaser

A 2,000-tonne grain barge had set sail from Lübeck in Germany and was making its way through the offshore gas field. Unknown to the standby vessels and surrounding manned production platforms, the Polish skipper had been enjoying a few drinks and was working on his computer with his back to the direction of travel. He also failed to see the unmanned gas platform loom out of the distance, and with only 100 metres to spare, and radio warnings coming in from the standby vessels in the area, he attempted to steer the ship clear, striking a glancing blow to the platform. The crew of the vessel leapt into the sea; last to jump/fall was the drunken skipper. The vessel made a big dent in the rig, which was shut down and vented for safety, followed by the barge sinking some 12 hours later. All of the crew on the barge were saved, and the skipper went on to serve a good few months in jail. Those few drinks turned out to be quite costly!

Tommy's Tale

Tommy had been out to scope his next job, which was the visual inspection of an Emergency Shutdown valve. He'd located the valve and conducted a quick survey along with one of the guys, who was going to assist him if it needed cleaning up. Going by the last inspection report, the photos taken the previous year showed quite a bit of scale (rust), and he expected it to be even more weathered this time around.

They took a few minutes to see what tools they would need and if any of the areas to be inspected were at height prior to making their way back to fill in the permit and all the other reams of paperwork that would be expected of them. Before they headed back to their desk in the Temporary Refuge Area (TRA), they located the nearest phone to where they would be working as well as the eye-wash station and MAC point, as these would all need to be referenced on the toolbox talk record sheet.

With the survey complete, they both headed back to the TRA to make a start on the paperwork. The route back took them through one of the process modules, and it was in here that Tommy noticed that one of the small bore process lines was glistening where all the surrounding area was dry and covered in the usual dust and corrosion. He took a closer look at the line (pipe) above and spotted a slow but steady drip coming from a Small Bore Connection (SBC) valve. The double block and bleed (two small valves with a sample point) appeared OK, and the valves were all closed, so they were obviously passing process fluids. Tommy asked his mate to go to the nearby spill kit and place some absorption pads in the fluid to soak it up and prevent it spreading whilst he contacted the control room. They agreed to meet up in the TRA once they had both taken care of their respective tasks. Tommy gloated that he'd probably get a safety award for this and told his mate not to expect anything for just putting a few pads down on the deck.

Tommy phoned the control room and explained what he had found and the actions taken. The Control Room Operator (CRO) said he would send one of the operators out to look and he'd meet them in the TRA. Tommy headed straight for the TRA where he laid it on thick to his pal, telling him that he'd probably get a medal for it as well, to go with the cash vouchers that were often given as safety awards.

Tommy hadn't spent his entire working life offshore. Prior to starting work on the rigs, he'd served with the Royal Marines, during which time he did a bit of boxing and was quite a handy little fighter. Everyone thought his flattened nose was from his time in the ring but it was actually the result of being suspected of cheating whilst playing Spoof, a well-known drinking game in the corps. The old hand he was up against thought he was being scammed, so he stopped the game by knocking Tommy out with a quick jab, breaking his nose and putting him on his arse.

Sitting in the TRA, they both waited for the operator to come over and made a start on the paperwork. In the corner of the room there was a radio-charging station, and it soon became apparent that one of the radios had been left turned on.

The radio crackled into life, and the voice of the CRO came over the net for one of the operators. The operator acknowledged and replied, "Pass your message."

The CRO then came back on the net. "Could you head over to the TRA please, mate, and meet up with Tommy the inspector. He's spotted a small leak, and he'll show you where it is if you could check it out."

During this time, Tommy's chest puffed out and he rubbed his thumb against his forefinger as a gesture indicating the cash vouchers he was going to get. He also went on to pretend to pin a medal to his chest when the radio kicked back into life: "Which one is Tommy? Is he the big tall inspector?"

Tommy pointed at his mate and shook his head and continued to pin on his imaginary medal. Then the CRO replied "No, mate, Tommy is the little ugly one with the flat nose… looks like he'd have a trophy cabinet full of silver boxing medals!"

Tommy's face dropped. The operator then came back on the radio laughing, "Of course, now I know who you mean, face like a slapped arse!"

He wasn't laughing when he arrived at the TRA and saw the look on Tommy's face! But Tommy's mate was laughing that hard he was about to have a leak of his own.

Inbetweenie

"It was only my second trip offshore, and it was on a different platform to my first trip, so I had to have an induction by the safety advisor before I could do anything. I was quite literally met by the safety advisor straight off the chopper and told to get into my PPE (Personal Protective Equipment). He pointed out the tea shack and told me to wait for him in there.

I was still as keen as mustard and remembered all of the rules from my first offshore trip, so I felt I had bit of a head start when going offshore for the second time. The safety advisor came in and grabbed a quick cuppa whilst he explained the company's golden safety rules to me before heading out onto the park (process area) for a quick tour of the complex. One of the main rules on any offshore platform was to hold onto the handrail when climbing or descending stairs; my hand instinctively grabbed onto the handrail just about everywhere we went. The safety officer was in a bit of a rush and seemed to be bounding up and down stairs as he showed me the key areas of the platform. On one descent, my hand was sliding down a handrail with a small gap in it as indicated by warning tape and a sign. I was concentrating on what the safety officer was saying and failed to spot the tape. My finger went into the gap but my body kept descending the stairs until my index finger snapped in two.

My safety induction was abruptly ended, my fingers were strapped together and I was painfully suited up (in my survival suit) sat waiting for the second crew change helicopter to fly me back to Norwich.

This, my second offshore trip of my new career, was planned to be for three weeks, but it only lasted a total of four hours. My planned two weeks' leave was extended to four weeks until I could pass my return-to-work medical.

Being a contractor, in total I received one day's pay in seven weeks... as obviously it was all my fault!"

CHAPTER 16

Pandemic

(The below text was written prior to the Covid-19 pandemic)

A pandemic is the worldwide spread of a new disease, and as such most people have no immunity to it. As an example, most of the fatal cases of the H1N1 virus were young people, unlike the common seasonal influenza viruses that would impact the older generation the hardest.

In the past, the UK offshore industry has had to plan and prepare for such flu pandemics and run trials and various models to ascertain the impact one would have on UK oil and gas production. The Offshore Pandemic Steering Group was set up by Oil & Gas UK with a number of key organisations, operators and service companies as well as various onshore authorities. Consideration was given to the loss of workforce through illness and death with planning assumptions based on a 30% and 50% loss of workforce throughout the UK sector. It was deemed that a 30% loss of workforce would generally allow continued production; however, at 50% the general opinion was that production would not be possible or at best significantly reduced.

Various problems needed to be addressed by the steering group, such as health screening at the heliports and the reception of infected personnel onshore as well as onward travel. Over recent years, guidance has had to be taken very seriously on swine flu and influenza.

In 2009, the industry ran a tabletop exercise involving 40 organisations as well as government agencies with the aim of learning as much in advance of any real potential pandemic threat.

Unlike a pandemic threat of influenza, the common seasonal flu can be anticipated with an annual flu vaccine. Most offshore companies in the UK will offer this to all members of their workforce, and it can be administered by the medic during the worker's offshore trip.

Teatime Teaser

The weather had been shocking for days, the sea had been pretty wild and the resupply vessels were unable to come alongside to safely deliver fresh water. It was winter, and the medic was pushing his campaign of hand hygiene and the need for correct hand washing.

OIM on the tannoy system to all personnel: "This is the OIM speaking. You are all aware of the requirement for prolonged hand washing to ensure good hygiene levels are maintained. However, due to the current water shortage, if we continue to run taps and use water at the current rate, I will have no option other than to de-man the platform to essential personnel only. The medic will therefore ensure hygiene gel dispensers are available at key locations and showering is restricted to five minutes. The laundry is closed until further notice."

A platform de-man for operational reasons meant that non-essential personnel were either sent home early on full pay or relocated to a hotel… and that is exactly why, following the OIM's announcement, every tap was mysteriously found turned on in full flow!!

A manager should always know his workforce.

Tommy's Tale

The clocks were changed to wintertime, and the dark nights were rolling in earlier each day. Tommy thought back to his recent summer holiday, which was slowly becoming a distant memory with each passing trip. The platform medic was running a winter health campaign with 'coughs & sneezes spread diseases' posters everywhere as well as telling you how many times to sing happy birthday to yourself whilst washing your hands to ensure they were getting a long-enough clean.

The crew knew that, with the confined living conditions in the accommodation module, if one person went down with the lurgy it soon spread through the ranks. The witch hunt is then on to find out who it was that brought it out with them, but that person always blames someone else, who blames someone else and so on.

In addition to the campaign posters, there was also the annual signs up advertising that a flu jab was available as well as the medic giving a talk about the advantages of having it at every safety meeting and encouraging guys to call into the sickbay to receive the injection. Most of the crew were sure he was on a bonus payment for sticking as many people as he could. The crew countered this with rumours that the injection wasn't in your arm and that you were actually jabbed in the arse cheek, falsely adding that you suffer with the flu for a few days whilst your body adjusts. It was all lies, of course, but the guys like to stir the shit if given the chance.

Tommy's three-man team, however, were all for it. The main argument was that it delayed them going out onto the park for an extra 30 minutes, and of course they'd need a cuppa afterwards to settle their nerves, again all bullshit!

For a few days, Tommy was getting pestered by the other two guys. He was always busy and had a lot to organise, so he just told them to go and get it done but to stop nagging him. They thought Tommy was a bit needle shy and wanted to test the theory by getting him to go to the medic with them. After days of moaning and bitching, Tommy gave in. Enough was enough, he thought, it's easier just to get it done and get them out of his hair. Even when they got down to the sickbay, they kept on at him, saying they should all go in at once. Tommy hung around at the door, saying he'd wait his turn, but the lads kept on taking the piss and pushing his buttons, winding him up. In the end, Tommy and the guys went into the room.

The medic told one of the guys to roll his sleeve up, but the other guy intervened, saying "Why don't we all roll our sleeves up and you can quickly jab us one after the other. We can see who winces the most!"

The medic agreed and went along with the banter. He didn't care as long as he managed to administer three more flu vaccinations and he could get on with his day. Tommy wanted the same but was at breaking point with the comedy double act that kept mocking him.

The medic told the guys to roll their sleeves up, and the vaccines were lined up on the desk ready to go. Tommy then played his trump card. He quickly asked the medic if he could administer the jabs as he was a trained advanced first aider, and he'd appreciate the experience. No sooner had the medic agreed than Tommy picked up the first vaccine, removed the end cap and stabbed the needle into the arm of the one who had been bitching the loudest. The other guy rolled down his sleeve and made a sharp exit.

Tommy got his flu jab, followed by a few days of peace and quiet.

Inbetweenie

"Back in the early 90's, Saturday night on our rig was known as 'movie night'. Guys would bring VHS cassettes of the latest films, admittidley most of them were pirate copies and the quality was terrible, but it passed the time. We'd all gather in the TV lounge and whoever had brought the film out with them would be awarded the front seat.

Tommy had made it known during tea break that he had one of the latest raunchy thrillers with him and that he'd get things set up and ready for 7pm. He explained that he'd bought video camera whilst on leave, along with a tripod. He borrowed a new VHS film from a friend, played it through is VHS recorder and filmed his TV screen to make a copy. He assured us that the quality was actually pretty good!

Movie time came and we all settled in with Tommy sat front and centre, as per the deal. The movie started and as promised the quality wasn't too bad. The film itself certainly lived up to its genre and in one early scene things started to get a little x-rated. It was at this point that the image started to appear distorted until it became apparent that it was actually the reflection of Tommy's television screen at home that could be seen on our big screen in the recreation room. At times the image became clearer and Tommy could be seen in the reflection clearly enjoying the film that his video camera was recording at home.....he was enjoying it a lot!

So here was Tommy now, sat in our recreation room, surrounded by 25-30 guys and gals offshore whilst there is a clear image of his reflection on the screen, showing him at home on his sofa with his trousers down enjoying himeself.

I've never seen anyone scramble for the remote control as fast as he did that day, or turn that shade of red!"

CHAPTER 17

Construction

Platform jackets and modules are built in large construction yards in various locations around the world, with the final build and commissioning location often being hundreds of miles away. The jacket structure can be fabricated and welded in one yard whilst the topside modules area assembled in multiple other yards. The entire structure is brought together for transportation as one single topside structure to the offshore location or assembled on site out at sea. The jacket and topsides are often floated offshore separately where the jacket would be sunk into position and secured to the seabed by piles prior to the topsides being lifted by a heavy barge lift crane (some of the largest cranes in the world) and secured onto the jacket.

These projects are huge feats of engineering, an example being the West Chirag platform in Azerbaijan, where the topsides alone weighed 19500 tonnes with up to 4000 people involved in the construction process, totalling around 20 million man hours of work. When in position, the West Chirag topsides comprised the heaviest structure to have been installed in the Caspian Sea.

Once in production, most installations have a construction department on board. These tend to be contracted companies that are tasked with installing new projects and carrying out structural repairs (particularly on older assets). The construction department would often work alongside the maintenance department to provide engineering support with various skills such as welding, electrical engineering, pipe fitting, fabricating and painting, and in turn these would be supported by a scaffolding or rope access company, where access might be required at height.

Teatime Teaser

I was running a team of guys on a platform off of the west coast of Africa. We'd been told that there were seats on the helicopter the next morning, and they were ours unless the scaffolders managed to get finished that same day, in which case they had first dibs.

The scaff foreman told us quite clearly not to bother packing our bags as we wouldn't be going anywhere. I'd seen their worksite and they had a scaffold platform to dismantle that was on the underside of the platform and therefore all classed as over-the-side work. There was no way they were going to get that stripped and all the equipment back on deck, not to mention packing it all for backload. I continuously ribbed the guy all that morning as he didn't stand a chance, although I couldn't help but admire his calm sense of assurance that they'd get it done.

Towards the end of the morning, I met him on the main deck from where we could just see the corner of his scaffold. One of his guys was in a lifejacket and harness clipped into the fall-arrest reel shouting across to the other as they coordinated the work.

I couldn't resist one more dig. "So how's it going, then? Making good progress I see," I said in the most sarcastic tone that I could muster as I gestured towards his lads and the largely untouched scaffold.

At that exact same point, we both watched as the entire structure fell to the sea below. One loud splash and within a few seconds there was no sign of it.

"Not bad," he said. "Now you'll have to excuse me. I've got to go and pack my bags!"

They really wanted to get home.

Tommy's Tale

It had been a long three months leading up to this point, but the large construction project that Tommy and his mate had been part of was coming to an end. The oil company had arranged a party for the 800 people who had been involved throughout the process and had invited everyone to attend one of the high-end hotels in Ulsan, South Korea.

The FPSO that had been under construction was destined for Angola so the guests of honour included Angolan dignitaries, diplomats and tribal leaders as well as the oil company's European and African senior management.

In recognition of everyone's efforts, the oil company had arranged presents for all the guests, all that is apart from Tommy and his mate. It soon became apparent that only 798 gifts had arrived and the two rope access Team Leaders were destined to leave the party empty handed.

In no time at all, the free bar was open and the champagne was on tap. Tommy and his oppo' were making the most of the liquid consolation gifts, the gifts that just kept on giving. This became more apparent when they somehow found their way into a storeroom and managed to change into some local clothing that they deemed to be fancy dress and in no time at all were leading the YMCA on the stage. Both as pissed as farts and dancing like they were on fire at that awkward early part of the evening when everyone else was just starting to loosen off their ties and relax.

As the night went on and the party atmosphere faded, the two of them were joined by one of the managers from site. They all decided enough was enough, and they made their way towards the exit of the hotel, only to stumble across a display cabinet next to the red carpet that was housing a selection of Angolan tribal masks. On closer examination, the cabinet was found to be unlocked, allowing them to examine the masks closer and even try them on for size. From this moment on,

Tommy's memory all gets a bit hazy. The alcohol had fully kicked in, and it was all a blackout from there until the sound of a phone ringing next to his ear, which brought him back to earth with a banging headache. Tommy fumbled around for his phone as he peeled back his eyelids, and to his relief, he had made it back to his digs. On the other end of the phone was a very distressed-sounding manager, the one who was with them last night. He went on to explain that he had been called very early by the senior oil company rep, who was demanding to know where the ancient masks were that had been loaned in good faith to the oil company by the Angolan tribal leaders.

Tommy denied any knowledge; in fact, he had little knowledge or recollection of anything beyond the free bar. With that, he hung up the phone and rolled over in bed to come face to face with a hideous mask that for an instant scared the shit out of him. Tommy quickly phoned his partner in crime, who confirmed he had the other mask staring at him from the bedside cabinet.

Tommy had no option but to phone the manager back and confess that they both had the masks. Tommy's confession did little to calm his nerves as he was informed that the vice president of the oil company had been contacted whilst on holiday by the Angolan ambassador, who demanded to know where the very old and incredibly valuable masks were.

The only option open to Tommy now was to contact the Korean site manager, confess to the drunken crime and explain that the masks would be returned shortly. Tommy and his sidekick jumped in a cab and made their way into his office, where he had also been summoned to on his day off by the oil company's vice president. Tommy soon realised just how serious this shit was but thankfully in time it would become overshadowed by the oil company's realisation that they had run over budget for the project by millions of dollars. The masks were safely reunited with their owners, the entire issue rapidly moved down the list of fuck-ups, and the two amigos lived to drink another day.

Tommy was intrigued, however, as to why the manager had originally been pulled in over the theft and not Tommy and his mate. The manager explained how they were captured on CCTV doing 'The Conga' as they headed out through the lobby.

"Strange that you just got the phone call, when they have all of our numbers?" asked Tommy. "Because you were both wearing the fucking masks!" the manager snapped.

It was then that Tommy realised that they could have got away with it, had he not confessed.

Inbetweenie

"I was working on a dive support vessel and realised that we had a new start on board. The vessel had a 'moon pool' built into the structure of the hull. A moon pool is an access point to the sea in the centre of the vessel where divers, equipment or tools can be lowered directly into the sea below.

It was a cracking summer's day, and the sea was as calm as a mill pond. The vessel was on station and holding perfectly still. I noticed the new start was standing with a hose pipe directing the water into the moon pool. I assumed he was using it to wash down the surrounding structure and swill the standing waste water into the sea. After an hour had passed, I walked back along the same route to find him still standing there holding the pipe. I noticed an audience had gathered at the bridge above. I couldn't resist asking the young lad what he was doing.

He shrugged his shoulders and told me he was filling up the moon pool, but it was taking some time.

'It will do, that's the North Sea in there pal, it's a bit bigger than your average garden pond!'

He didn't get my point, bless him! He was still there when I walked by some ten minutes later.

CHAPTER 18

The Drilling Crew

When in full operation, the drill floor is one of the most hazardous working environments in the offshore world. Offshore drilling operations involve the use of heavyweight and high-torque rotating equipment coupled with immense amounts of stored energy. The 24/7 operation is manned by a team of multi-skilled Drillers, all of whom must have a keen eye on safety whilst operating in arduous physical conditions around the clock.

The Roustabouts do the labour-intensive work, keeping the drilling area in good working order, offloading supplies and assisting the Roughnecks. The Roughnecks carry out the skilled labour such as adding drill lengths and maintaining and operating the equipment on the drill floor. The Derrickman works at height often 20 to 30 metres above the drill floor and operates equipment as directed by the Driller and Assistant Driller (AD). The Driller controls the operation on the drill floor, such as the speed of the drill and weight of the top drive force onto the drill, all with assistance from the AD. The entire operation is overseen by the Toolpusher, who ensures all procedures are being followed and that the entire operation is run safely and efficiently. He also liaises directly with the oil company to ensure the client's requirements are being fulfilled where possible.

Teatime Teaser

I was new on the drill crew and one of the last to arrive at the heliport for my check-in. I naively left my bags with the guys whilst I went to the toilets. As soon as I got back, we were called to check-in, and from there we carried our bags through to security. My bag was scanned, and I was quickly taken to one side by security and asked if I had packed the bag myself. I nodded. The airport security then opened my bag to reveal a long object wrapped in aluminium baking foil. He opened up the foil to reveal a bright pink dildo.

"Taking some company with you, I see, sir?"

Tommy's Tale

The drill crew had been mobilised to the rig and were preparing for the drilling programme that was scheduled to start in the next few days. Equipment checks, maintenance and offloading of supplies had been keeping them busy so far, but things would get a whole lot busier once they commenced drilling around the clock. Yesterday, most of the afternoon was spent cleaning the place up as there was to be a visit by the company man (oil company representative) and the new onshore-based manager from the drilling company. The Toolpusher also made it known that there would be a new start joining the squad the following day and that he was to be shown the ropes and kept safe whilst he settled in.

The crew started their shift the following day and continued ensuring all the equipment was in good working order prior to the management team paying them a visit. The Toolpusher asked for everyone to be assembled on the drill floor at 11:00, giving the management time to have their induction, having just arrived by helicopter that morning. He also asked Tommy to ensure the new lad made it to the drill floor ready for the management meeting.

At about 10:45, Tommy made his way to the drill floor and on arrival suddenly realised he'd forgotten all about the green hat (the new guy) that he was supposed to be looking after but was relieved to see amongst the gaggle of grease and drill mud-coloured overalls there was a bright orange pair of overalls topped with a shiny new green V-Gard helmet. "That's my new guy right there," Tommy thought as he went over and introduced himself.

As the new guy was stood right in front of Tommy and they were all just waiting for the management visitors to make their appearance, Tommy was handed a pot of grease. This was followed shortly by an open box of bright-yellow ear plugs. Tommy knew what had to be done. One at a time he took an earplug from the box and dabbed its end into the grease. He then gently stuck in on top of the new lad's helmet. The foam earplugs are so light they stick in place very easily with the grease, and provided the assailant has a gentle touch he can repeat the process countless times, with the aim being to fill the new lad's green helmet with bright-yellow foam nobbles for no other reason than to make him look a twat.

Tommy tried to contain his laughter as too did the rest of the lads. The key was to see how long it would take for the victim to realise the new look he was modelling. After a few minutes of sniggering, the crew's mutterings all fell quiet as the Toolpusher made his way onto the drill floor followed by two men in spotless brand-new overalls. "That'll be the company man and our new senior manager," Tommy thought.

The Toolpusher had barely looked up at the squad as he called out a name and at the same time gestured for one of the guys who he'd brought with him to go and join the rest of the drill crew. The Toolpusher then looked up from his clipboard at the same time the guy in front of Tommy heard his name and stepped forward whilst also being introduced as the new Aberdeen-based manager who was essentially running the show. He stepped clear of the crew with his helmet looking like some kind of prop from the film *Hellraiser*. The drill crew were all chuckling away to themselves whilst the Toolpusher was going into an absolute meltdown. Tommy had nailed the wrong man; in fact, he couldn't have nailed it more wrong if he'd tried. The guy the Toolpusher had brought with him was the new start that Tommy was meant to be looking after. He'd fucked up on two counts as the Toolpusher soon worked out who was responsible for the headwear decoration that was now being modelled by his new boss.

The Toolpusher quickly got a replacement helmet from the doghouse (drill floor control room) and handed it to the manager. The manager laughed off the prank and set about his little speech as if nothing had happened. Tommy, however, saw that he was deeply in the shit as he stood there listening to what the manager had to say whilst feeling the Toolpusher's glare burning holes in the side of his face.

For Tommy, this was the start of a very long day.

Inbetweenie

"One of the guys had gone into the gym and hopped on the bike to get some training in. He found himself in there alone, which made a nice change from the knuckle draggers who normally went in to throw heavy weights around and fart whilst admiring themselves in the mirror. As he also had the responsibility of maintaining the gym equipment he took the opportunity to glance over at the treadmill and looked at the running belt to check on its condition. He did this whilst still pedalling away and listening to his music through his headphones. He decided to reach over, start up the treadmill and ramp it up to max speed to see how the belt was running and if any adjustments were required.

Unbeknownst to him, another of the guys entered the gym behind him who was also wearing headphones and hopped straight onto the treadmill, which was going at full tilt. His feet quite literally needed to hit the ground running, but this was never going to happen, and he was instantly ejected off the machine and thrown against the backwall, dislocating a finger in the process... I stepped through the door into the gym at the exact time the hamster stepped onto the wheel and watched him fly past me!"

CHAPTER 19

Emergency Response Team

Each offshore installation must have the facilities, equipment and trained personnel to respond to and manage emergencies. These can include fires, explosions, confined space incidents, casualties at height and more.

The initial training for an Offshore Emergency Response Team Member (OERTM) is around 36 hours with further training required every two years at an OPITO-approved training centre. The teams must also carry out regular training exercises offshore to familiarise themselves with the equipment and environment.

Typically, the team size will range from four to six emergency team members with an appointed Offshore Emergency Response Team Leader (OERTL). The emergency team are trained in incident response, casualty recovery, Search and Rescue (SAR) and the use of BA, firefighting equipment and extinguishing media.

During an incident, the emergency team are deployed under the direction of the OIM, who will be based in the Emergency Control Centre (ECC). They will work and train closely with the platform medic, who may also deploy to the scene depending on the nature of the emergency.

Teatime Teaser

I was on a helideck firefighting training course when one of the lads on my team had entered the burning helicopter to fight the internal fire. We'd all been briefed by the instructor on exactly what to do: who would be operating the foam branch to lay down a protective blanket, who would be cooling the aircraft fuselage with the monitor and who would be the entry team to extinguish the internal cabin fire. My mate was on the water hose and bragged how he was the hero of the hour, bursting into the cabin in BA and saving everyone on board.

However, when the foam blanket was laid and the fuselage cooled, his moment of fame consisted of tripping on the door ledge, falling face first into the internal straw fire and dropping his hose on full jet, which flailed around until it hit him clean in the bollocks, causing what we later learnt were officially classed by the hospital A&E as 'extensive testicular injuries.'

The 'hero of the hour' was actually rescued by the rest of the team and once recovered, had to attend the course again.

Tommy's Tale

It was around 8:00 and the muster alarm sounded on the platform, followed shortly after by the familiar voice of the OIM.

"Attention all personnel, this is the OIM. This is a drill; this is a drill. Please don warm clothing and proceed to your primary muster point."

At this time, most of the crew headed to their respective muster points, one being in the galley and the other in the recreation room. The muster controller carries out a roll call to establish if everyone is present. The Control Room Operators (CROs) remain where they are to monitor the process and automated emergency systems. There are a team of coordinators along with the OIM that muster in the ECC to manage the muster or emergency scenario. From here, the OIM has communications with all parties including the emergency contacts in the head office in Aberdeen and any emergency services or agencies based onshore that may be required, such as the coastguard. The emergency team muster at their designated point, carry out checks on all of their equipment and ready themselves to deploy at the request of the OIM.

Tommy made his way direct to the emergency team muster point and established communications with the ECC, notifying them that the team were all accounted for and ready. As this was clearly a drill, the team just donned their fire-suit bottoms and boots and waited on an update.

Tommy heard the muster controllers reporting in: "ECC,

muster point one."

"Muster point one, ECC. Pass your message."

"ECC, this is muster point one. I have a head count of 34, three four. Missing one, over."

"Muster point one, this is ECC, message received, you are missing one. Break Break. Emergency team, this is ECC."

"ECC, pass your message," stated Tommy, knowing exactly what was coming next.

"Emergency team, ECC. The head count is incorrect; we are missing one person. Please proceed to muster point one and enquire with his room buddy as to where he was last seen."

With that, Tommy slipped on his fire tunic and made his way into muster point one. The room was filled with the normal drone of chit chat that soon fell silent when Tommy asked the occupant of cabin 231 to come forward. After a brief chat, the missing party's room-mate explained that he had been for a shower and given the thumbs-up signalling that he was all done and that the cabin was his. The last he had seen of him was when he left the recreation room and headed up for his shower. The volume at the muster point went back up when a few people overheard the response, and it spread around the room like wildfire.

Tommy avoided the overuse of the radio and picked up the phone to explain to the OIM where the last whereabouts of the missing guy was. No sooner had he put the phone down than the OIM's voice kicked in again over the PA system.

"Attention all personnel, this is the OIM. The head count is incorrect, we are missing one person. The emergency team are carrying out a sweep of the accommodation to establish his location. Please remain at your muster point until further notice."

By this time, Tommy had rounded up his emergency team and made their way up to level 2, where he met the medic. The joint team then headed along the corridor to cabin 231. Given the nature of the situation, Tommy did away with the formality of knocking on the door, he just opened it and burst straight in, followed sharply by the medic.

They were greeted by the sight of a naked man laid on the bed in a darkened room illuminated by the dim glow of his laptop comuter which was displaying wide-screen porn, the sound for which was booming through his noise-cancelling headphones. The laptop was hurled onto the floor in sheer panic as the sight of Tommy and the lads bursting in like the SAS had completely put him off his stroke.

The muster excercie was soon drawn to a close by the OIM putting out another tanoy. "Attention all personnel, this is the OIM. The head count is correct, all personnel can now stand down. Could Mr 'Smith' first wash your hands and then report to my office immediately!"

Inbetweenie

"It was getting towards the end of the trip, and one of the guys had made it known from day one that he was on a fitness campaign with the view to losing weight. He went to the gym every night after shift and claimed to be watching his diet, although we all knew otherwise as he was often seen balls-deep in the strawberry ice cream claiming it was one of his 'five a day'.

On the last day of our trip we all boarded the aircraft for our flight home, with Mr Weight Watcher being the last man on. The aircraft lifted from the deck, hovered for a few seconds and then lowered back to the deck. The engines ramped up again and attempted another lift. This happened three times in total before the aircraft finally settled and the pilot announced that we needed to lose some weight from the payload. The HLO approached the aircraft cabin door and Mr Weight Watcher was escorted from the helicopter and off the helideck, something of a walk of shame given his claimed efforts to have slimmed down. Once the helideck was clear, the HLO gave the pilot the thumbs-up, the engines ramped back up to speed and we headed skywards with no issue at all.

Mr Weight Watcher arrived home the following day and didn't mention his diet again."

CHAPTER 20

Offshore Installation Manager

The Offshore Installation Manager (OIM) holds the most senior management position on the platform with the main responsibility being to ensure the health, safety and welfare of all personnel on board by ensuring full compliance with all mandatory regulations and procedures.

The manager must be aware of all hazardous activities that are being carried out on the installation and ensure they are being performed in a safe manner with all risk reduced to as low as reasonably practicable (ALARP). The OIM's role is vital in an emergency, and therefore they must attend an OPITO-certified Major Emergency Management Initial Response training course. This training provides the skill sets in an emergency to identify the problem, determine the correct level of response and ensure that the correct actions are carried out. Events need to be anticipated, a plan formulated and the emergency management team must support the manager's decisions and act accordingly.

Teatime Teaser

When you're an OIM and you walk into your office during the evening to find the new night-shift steward sat back in your chair, feet up on your desk, eating the bag of sweets that your wife gave you as a little offshore treat. He's using your office phone during his break time, he has no idea who you are and looks up from his call and says "Give me five minutes, mate. The wife's giving me a right bollocking here!"

"Tell her to relax and put the phone down. I'll take it from here!"

Tommy's Tale

Tommy was all set to head out for work. He'd been out of the cabin 10 minutes but suddenly realised that he'd forgotten his fleece top, an essential third layer when wearing a survival suit on the flight. He quickly knocked on the door and opened it. The door clattered into the open toilet door that was swung into the room. His roommate was still in there using the sink and brushing his teeth. It's perfectly accepted to expect to be given at least 10 minutes of peace at that time in the morning, so he greeted his returning roommate with "Fuck off and leave me alone, will ya!!" Tommy just laughed, grabbed his fleece and headed up to heli-admin ready for his flight.

It had been a long day, and the satellite maintenance team had just returned to the main asset following a day of servicing a generator on a nearby NUI. Like most guys offshore, Tommy wore many hats aside from his trade as he was also a HLO (Helicopter Landing Officer) and banksman. The role of HLO came with other training requirements such as Dangerous Goods by Air, HSE-approved First Aid, CAA VHF Radio Licence and Helideck Emergency Response Team Leader. There was definitely a 'Jack of all trades, master of fuck all' feel about the way the industry was going. With each course you attended, there was always a mention of the legal implications or threat of court action if you got it wrong. Today was one of those days when Tommy had got it wrong, and he knew he was going to get a kick up the arse; he just didn't know how hard or who from.

En route to the unmanned satellite earlier that day, Tommy was HLO and therefore seated behind the pilot and ready to exit the aircraft first to take control of the helideck when they arrived. He would watch as the OIM for the day made his way down to check on the platform systems. Tommy would also supervise his HDAs unloading the baggage and freight. Once the aircraft was clear of freight and passengers and the OIM was happy that the platform was safe, the HLO would give a thumbs-up and release the aircraft. On this occasion, Tommy had failed to complete one of his duties which was to ensure all of the lifejackets that had been worn by the disembarked passengers were bagged up and back on the aircraft. The OIM gave him the thumbs-up, a signal that the platform was safe to man for the day. Tommy stepped down from the helideck, double-clicked his radio transmit button to get the captain's attention and signalled to the pilot that the aircraft was clear to lift. Tommy followed protocol and watched as the aircraft went into a hover, then dipped its nose and headed out over the sea. The landing gear raised and the noise of the engines faded as it headed into the clouds above. Tommy's heart then sank as he turned around to spot a bag of lifejackets sitting there, a bag that he knew was essential to the aircraft's onward routing and passengers. Tommy clicked his radio mike and transmitted a very timid message requesting that the aircraft return and land to collect the forgotten items. The pilots weren't impressed and nor was Tommy's OIM when he informed him of the cock-up. The aircraft operators lodged a complaint with the onshore logistics team, and in turn the issue was relayed offshore to the field manager, who would be waiting to speak to Tommy later that day.

Back on the main platform, the OIM had taken a call from the logistics team in Aberdeen to report the cock-up, and they requested that Tommy be briefed on the correct procedures prior to clearing an aircraft for departure from the helideck.

Later that day, the manager heard the team return to the platform and the helicopter depart for the beach (Norwich Aiport). He was going to put a tannoy out for Tommy to report to his office, but he'd been at his desk for a while and thought he'd stretch his legs and go and pay him a visit in his cabin.

When Tommy got back from the platform, he opted to grab a shower and freshen up. It had been a shitty day working in the confines of the generator, and although it was only a short flight back, he'd been sweating buckets in his survival suit and three layers of clothing. Tommy stepped out of the shower, towel wrapped around his waist at the exact time that the OIM knocked on his door and stepped in. As per earlier in the day, the outer door rattled against the open shower door, only this time Tommy was stood there. The OIM peered around the door to be greeted by Tommy, who had his back to him and thought it was his roommate coming back. He flung his towel to the floor and spun around bollock naked, to repeat back what had been shouted at him earlier in the day: "Fuck off and leave me alone, will ya!!"

"My office in 10 minutes, we need to talk!"

Tommy had a lame excuse lined up for the now minor issue of the life jackets, but he couldn't account for exposing himself to the field manager whilst telling him to fuck off.

Inbetweenie

"We were doing some work on the crane at height above the main deck. There was a new guy sent out to join me, and it was his first trip offshore. Prior to climbing the ladders from the main deck, I told him that we would pull our tool bag up on a rope. I pointed out the rope to him, which could be seen coiled and secured to the handrail next to the top of the ladder. I explained to him that when the rope was thrown down, simply tie the end of the rope to the bag, and I would haul it up. Just as

I was about to climb the ladders, the OIM appeared and asked to have a quick chat with me about the task. I gestured for my green-hat colleague to head up onto the access platform, and we would reverse roles for this simple task.

The OIM smiled at the new guy and explained that he'd stick around to see how he was settling in. He watched as the young lad scaled the ladder, and I explained to the OIM how we were going to haul up the tool bag. No sooner had I finished explaining when there was a loud thud at the OIM's feet. He'd only gone and untied the rope from the handrail, before throwing the entire coil down to the deck below where it landed in a shitty heap.

The OIM looked down at the pile of rope at his feet, then looked up at the young lad, who was by this time scratching his head trying to figure out how this was going to work.

'He's not quite grasped the concept of hauling, has he?'"

CHAPTER 21

Training and Meetings

With the increase in health and safety and restrictions on manning, most offshore workers have to attend a variety of training courses to cover multiple roles. There is a requirement for workers to receive ongoing information, instruction and training to ensure they remain competent to complete the many roles and responsibilities that are expected of them whilst offshore.

In most instances, courses and meetings have to be attended during leave time. This then removes the requirement to provide cover for a worker who is taken off shift. Any person providing cover would also need the required qualifications and experience. In many cases, such people are hard to find.

Refresher courses can range anywhere from one to five days long and in some cases even longer. This then has a big impact on a workers' leave time. The very much sought-after two or three weeks' leave can suddenly be cut down dramatically, and this can be expected multiple times throughout the year, depending on how many qualifications the individual holds.

For those who have to attend meetings, the same issue arises as for most the meeting won't be held close to home and there is an expectation to travel. A simple three or four hour meeting can result in a worker giving up two days' leave when taking travel and the need for an overnight stay into account.

Teatime Teaser

We were doing our offshore survival refresher training and had reached the stage where we had to complete the helicopter capsize drills in the pool. One of the lads was clearly a non-swimmer, and the instructors were doing a great job of reassuring him that he would be 'just fine'. "But what if the window doesn't open?" "What happens if I get stuck?" "I feel a bit sick!"

The instructors continued with their calming approach, taking him to one side and reminding him that he'd done it before and that there was nothing to worry about. They let him watch as group after group were rotated through the six-man simulator. He watched as its base slapped against the surface of the pool, then as it was lowered further, and the cabin filled with water, ingulfing the passengers. He saw everybody take a deep breath as the water level rose above their heads, and then the module capsized and rotated upside down. He observed as all the guys pushed out the windows next to them before releasing their seatbelts and pulled themselves through the opening, before popping up to the surface and inflating their life jackets.

I had completed my session, so I joined the others as we

stood poolside and watched as it was now his turn. He held his breath, smashed out his window prior to attempting to swim out whilst still strapped into his seat. His panic then fully set in as he hung upside down, frantically clawing away at his belt buckle. The rescue diver was by his side and managed to reach in and release the strap. The young lad then firmly planted his foot in the rescue diver's face, ripping of his mask and bursting his nose as he used his face as a springboard to launch himself to the surface.

The once calming instructor, now with a bleeding nose again took him to one side, only this time not as supportive as the previous occasion.

Tommy's Tale

Tommy's manager asked him to attend a meeting in Aberdeen during his time off. It was fairly short notice, but Tommy duly enquired what it was all about and who would be attending. He was told that there would be representatives from other platforms who he knew and saw this as an opportunity for a jolly. As such, he happily agreed to go.

When planning the trip, Tommy had no trouble booking his flights, but because of the short notice struggled to get a room in the hotel where his colleagues were staying, but he eventually managed to book a room not too far away from their hotel.

Tommy, being conscientious and wanting to create a good

impression, decided to travel up to Aberdeen the evening before the meeting to ensure that he was at the meeting venue in plenty of time the following morning. Unfortunately, Tommy's flight was delayed and got to his accommodation later than intended.

He eventually arrived at the hotel reception slightly weary and travel worn from his earlier delays, and he was greeted by a slightly subdued-looking member of the staff, who stated that the hotel was fully occupied and there had been an error with his booking. Tommy then pleaded with the receptionist to re-check, and as luck would have it, he was offered a room in the hotel's annex apartment building a short walk away. Not ideal, but having no choice, Tommy picked up his bags, and following the directions he'd been given and made his way to the other building. He found the building without effort, the keyless entry card (the building wasn't staffed) worked OK and as it turned out his room was quite tidy, happy days!

Tommy then attended the meeting the next day, followed by the obligatory meal in the evening and a few post-meal pints with his buddies to catch up. After a few more beers, a trip to the casino and a 3:00am finish, he headed back to his digs absolutely smashed but somehow managed to find his room.

At some point during the small hours, he woke up desperately needing to relieve himself of the post-meal beers. Somewhat disorientated but with a sense of urgency, Tommy made his way to the en-suite bathroom, found the door and stumbled in. It was at this point that he realised that he wasn't in the bathroom at all and was actually standing in the annex hallway, naked, just as the room door clicked closed behind him.

So now he was starting to sober up pretty rapidly, he realised that he was faced with two problems. He still had an urgent need to offload the evening's beer and he was also stranded bollock naked in a building that had no staff and no means of summoning assistance.

Fortunately, Tommy was from a military background and was taught to improvise to survive from an early age. Clearly these skills had not left him and he began to assess his options. Looking around him, Tommy spotted a set of curtains covering a window at the end of the hallway. He deduced that the curtains would make an ideal temporary garment.

The building was a typical Aberdeen town-centre building of grand construction, and this posed another issue for Tommy as the curtains were covering quite a large window and the curtain pole was at least eight feet off the ground. Not to be discouraged, he continued to survey his surroundings and spotted a table at the other end of the hallway. Tommy grabbed the table, positioned it in front of the window and climbed up to release a curtain. Almost mid-way through and with an increased sense of urgency, he lost his balance and began to fall backwards, grabbed the curtain to steady himself but continued to fall, pulling the entire arrangement with him and landing on the floor. The impact shocked his bladder, and in an instant it began to empty itself. As he was lying on his back, the fountain shot into the air, gradually easing as he and the curtains were soaked in urine.

Job done and feeling relieved, Tommy freed one of the large curtains, which he proceeded to don in a toga fashion.

Now suitably attired, he felt confident enough to make his way back to the hotel and seek assistance to get back into his room. Although looking like someone in Roman fancy dress and smelling like a tramp, he managed to convince himself that this was a credible explanation should anyone see him. Tommy then retraced his steps of the previous evening back to the hotel reception area.

Arriving at the hotel entrance, Tommy's sense of relief was short-lived as he found the doors locked and a sign advising that he should ring a bell to summon the night porter. He rang the bell and waited impatiently whilst trying to concoct a credible story for his present predicament and state of attire.

After a few minutes, a dishevelled night porter arrived and unlocked the door. He quietly looked Tommy over before asking calmly "Are those our curtains?"

Tommy nodded back. The porter replied "What room are you in?"

Tommy answered with his name and room. "You'd better come in then." Tommy entered reception, and the porter sorted another key before sending him back to his room.

In the morning, Tommy awoke, feeling hung over and having a vague recollection of a surreal bad dream where he was wandering naked around Aberdeen centre. He understandably felt relieved to find himself tucked up in bed securely in his room. After lying there for a few minutes, he eventually pulled himself round and began to climb out of bed. His feet landed in a urine-soaked curtain… and it all came flooding back to him.

Inbetweenie

"It was often said that I bore an uncanny resemblance to Steve, who was one of the other operators as well as a Helideck Assistant (HDA). If ever I needed to chat with Steve, I knew exactly how to catch him. All I had to do was listen out for a helicopter, and Steve was guaranteed to be on or around the helideck.

This was quite a few years ago and before helideck crews wore the fire suits and firefighting helmets of the modern-day attire, nor was there any radio communications between team members. Back then, it was just a two-man team that relied on hand signals and wearing dark-green overalls and a pair of earmuffs. Their appearance was no different to anyone else on the platform.

On this one particular day I wanted to have a chat with Steve, I heard a helicopter was on the helideck, so I made my way up to the passenger assembly point at the foot of the stairs leading to the helicopter. There were no passengers around, which meant that the aircraft must have been fully loaded and it would soon be lifting and heading back to the beach. I decided to make my way up a set of stairs which took me to one of two small viewing areas or firefighting pits. The second pit area was on the opposite side of the helideck, and given the wind direction I knew that the helideck crew would be over on that side of the helicopter. I could see that Steve was positioning the final few items in the aircraft's boot. He'd pretty much climbed all the way in and was laid on his stomach sliding the bags and freight into the depths of the stowage area.

The HLO was in the opposite pit and appeared to be looking at one of the fire monitors (fixed firefighting equipment that could be activated in an emergency). He glanced up at the exact time that I arrived on the opposite side of the helideck and gave me a wave. I naturally waved back. The next thing I knew, the HLO gave the pilot the thumbs-up. This was a signal that all was secure and he could lift off and head for home! In an instant, I realised that the HLO had mistaken me for his HDA and hadn't noticed Steve's black boots poking out of the rear of the aircraft. The engines ramped up and the helicopter started to lift! God only knows what must have been going through Steve's mind other than his feet could be seen kicking like crazy as he tried to escape the confines of the boot. The HLO spotted Steve and stood up, waving his arms frantically at the pilot, who immediately eased back on the throttles and allowed the helicopter to rest on the deck.

As for me, well, I kept an exceptionally low profile for the rest of the shift!"

CHAPTER 22

Standby

Throughout all offshore projects, there are times when personnel, equipment and logistics are on standby. This can be for a multitude of reasons and for varying lengths of time. If standby is an operational requirement, then most of the resources will be on full pay or hire even though they may be doing very little apart from remaining available and on call.

One of the most common reasons for standby for those mobilised offshore can be permit delays. For example, where hot work with spark potential such as welding is required in an area where there is currently a team working on open pipework and there is a potential for flammable liquids to be in the area or an explosive atmosphere, the hot work would be put on hold until the pipework was all secure and the area made safe.

Weather can also be a major factor and cause for project delays, resulting in teams and equipment being on standby especially where the sea state is concerned. A lot of the marine logistics and crane operations rely on maximum wave heights being within operating parameters. Vessels can stand off the platform for days on end waiting for the weather and sea state to settle. Often this can be critical when platforms require a fresh water or diesel resupply.

Platforms can choose not to fly workers offshore if there is a 'bed bust' or lack of beds to cater for the full workforce. In such cases, they can be checked into hotels and remain on the beach on pay waiting for work offshore to be finished and freeing up the much-needed beds.

Teatime Teaser

"I'd been on standby for 10 days, and with only four days of my two-week shift remaining, I was pretty confident that they wouldn't send me offshore at this stage of my rota. A couple of my mates were jetting off abroad for a week and asked if I wanted to go. The opportunity was too good to miss. Flight booked, bags packed, I was sat in the airport lounge having a few beers with the lads. It was at this point where my guard was down and not quite on the ball. My phone rang and I answered it to hear my boss say that as I was on full pay, he wanted me to attend the office for a meeting. Suddenly whilst on the call, the airport tannoy system sounded with a final boarding call for 'Mr Tommy' to make his way to the gate immediately for the Ibiza flight.

I had a great week in the sun but didn't get paid a penny for my two-week trip.

Oh, and they sacked me!"

Tommy's Tale

The drilling rig was waiting to bring a new caisson (essentially a huge section of steel tubing) on board, and the top drive was going to be used to lift the tubing from the vessel, which was standing outside of the platform's 500-metre zone due to the rough seas. The plan was for the vessel to reverse in and the caisson to be lifted from the deck into a vertical position under the cantilevered drill floor. The load would then be transferred onto static steel wires, securing in position by using a rope access team to place and remove shackles once the weight had been transferred.

Tommy was one of the Rope Access Techs who would be abseiling down and installing the shackles and then climbing clear until the weight was transferred across before returning on the ropes and removing the original and redundant slings and shackles.

The rope team had been mobilised for a simple two-day trip, and yet here they were 10 days later and still no sign of the weather calming down. Typical for the sun to be shining and the sea like glass on the day they landed offshore, only for the wind to whip up the next day. The guys had been briefed on the task; they had readied their equipment and completed all the risk assessments and permits, and were just waiting for them to be approved, giving them the green light to get the job done and get home.

There was no other work for them to do, so they simply remained on standby, drank tea and ate biscuits. Tommy shared a cabin with the other level 1 on the team, and the level 3 had a cabin to himself on the other side of the corridor. Whilst waiting over the last 10 days, the team got to know a lot about each other, and it always amazed Tommy how diverse the characters were that you could be working with from trip to trip. His roommate, it transpired, trained as a priest, but in the end threw it all in and starting working offshore. He had turned to God after having a random yet very vivid dream that he was going to be involved in an accident and knocked from his bike by a passing car. Unfortunately for him, the dream became reality, but he felt that he had been given a warning from above and so he turned to the church and his life changed.

Tommy heard this tale and with empathy stated, "Not sure I believe that pish, if you dreamt it then more likely it was a coincidence, but as long as your happy, pal, eh?"

A few nights had passed since hearing the tale when Tommy, who was fast asleep, was woken by his cabin mate, who screamed out and banged his head off the bunk. He'd obviously had one hell of a nightmare.

"Are you OK, pal?" Tommy enquired before settling back down and drifting back to sleep (with one eye partially open).

The next day over breakfast, Tommy asked what the nightmare was and admitted it put the shits up him as well.

"It was nothing you'd want to know about. Don't worry yourself about it," declared Tommy's mate, peering over his bowl of cornflakes.

"Worry myself? What do I need to worry myself over?" Tommy carried on probing away but wasn't getting any further info.

As the day went on so too did the banter as the part-trained priest was ribbed by Tommy for his godly visions and predictions. He even asked when the weather was going to settle and when would they be going home, but it was all laughed off. The wind did start to drop that day, and by early evening the sea state had come down to the point that the OIM wanted them to get the job done whilst the weather window allowed. The permit was soon signed on and the ropes rigged as per the plan. The level 3 Team Leader had a great vantage point as well as access to both sets of ropes in order to perform a rescue and lower the level 1s to the deck, some 25 metres below if required.

Both Tommy and his opposite numbers were in their harnesses and attached to independent ropes on opposite sides of a hatch which had a significant drop below. This was all still quite new to Tommy, so he was still feeling those last-minute jitters before leaning back and putting faith in his equipment to take the load. To ease his nerves and keep his mind occupied, Tommy continued to rib his mate about his nightmares and how he thought they could become reality. The joking escalated right up until the point when they were about to abseil over the edge, when Tommy suddenly asked what the last nightmare was about that had woken them both up.

"You don't want to know," came the reply.

"Yeah, I do. It's all a load of bollocks anyway. What was the dream about?"

"OK, you were standing right where you are now, and when you lean back to drop over the edge both of your ropes fail!" Tommy just stood staring at him in silence. "I woke up to the sound of you screaming, Tommy, just before you hit the deck!"

"What the fuck are you telling me this now for!" Tommy shouted.

With that, his mate leaned back over the edge and gently squeezed his descender handle as he slowly lowered himself into the void, and with a smile on his face shouted back, "Because you said it's all a load of bollocks, mate!"

Inbetweenie

"As a 'respected' member of the senior management team on board the platform, I was often working long hours with interspersed breaks and time away from the office when work allowed. I'd often get a quiet period mid-afternoon which fell between meetings, and I'd use this time to head to the gym for some much-needed training. At this time of day, the night shift were still sleeping and the day shift were still working, so the gym was all mine.

After a brief visit to my cabin to get changed, I headed into the gym. Sure enough, it was nice and quiet, the stereo was turned off and I was the only one in there. I stepped onto the treadmill and starting jogging whilst listening to my music via the Bluetooth headphones that I had recently bought.

As often is the case, the action of running and my body being active away from the desk loosened up a few bubbles of trapped wind. It took a few minutes for the cramps to subside, but I soon felt the relief as I let out a series of short farts, each one escaping everytime my feet struck the treadmill. There must have been about 10 of them, one after the other and I actually thought out loud, 'Aww, that's better!' although the smell was so bad it was almost making me gag.

No sooner had I finished my farting extravaganza, I noticed the lace in one of my trainers had come undone, so I stopped the treadmill and bent down to tie it up. Out of the corner of my eye, I spotted the safety advisor and turned fully to see a group of people who had entered the gym without my knowledge. They were being given a platform induction, and as platform manager these were the very same people due to meet me for an introduction meeting in my office later that day. This was going to be awkward!"

CHAPTER 23

Mobilisation

Mobilisation, or 'mob' and 'demob', are terms that refer to the travel time to and from the platform or installation. For some, this can mean a short taxi from home to the local heliport, or in more extreme cases it can involve days of travel with overnight stays en route. In such extreme cases, the mobilisation expenses will be built into the contract and paid for by the client. For domestic travel within the UK, the employing or contracting company will often cover the expense of a second-class rail fare and pay the equivalent. For many this is more often not the case and the individual will find himself invariably paying more that the allotted travel allowance, especially in more recent times of austerity and low oil prices.

For most employees and contractors, their rate of pay does not start until they actually check in at their departure heliport, so any delays in transport such as late trains or cancelled flights can cost the individual dearly. With this in mind, workers will often travel the day previous and pay for an additional night in a hotel rather than risk the chance of losing a day's wages. Although the offshore rotations are generally two weeks on and two weeks off, it's clear to see that travel time soon eats into the worker's leave period.

Teatime Teaser

As an ad hoc offshore worker, you never really knew when the next job was going to come your way, and as such never really wanted to turn work down. The guys arranging the contracts knew this and were always looking to cut corners, save money and in general just fuck us about. We weren't employees; we were just numbers that could fill the gaps without commitment from the employing company.

I was once offered a two-week trip offshore. After some debate, I eventually agreed a rate and made my way to Aberdeen to pick a few things up from the stores before making my way to the heliport for my flight to the rig. I was just about to pop into the office to speak to the guy who had mobilised me when I heard him telling someone that the client had asked for the team to be cut down. I soon worked out that I was on that team, so I waited around the corner in earshot to hear at first-hand how such executive discussions play out.

"How many guys do you have to bump?" asked Mr Random.

"Two," came the reply from Mr Mobiliser. "Tommy (that's me) will be one of them. He's a right greedy twat who pestered me for more money."

I heard others in the office giggling away at his smart-arse remark, and at that point, my blood boiled, and I walked around the corner.

Mr Mobiliser looked up. "Sorry, mate, can I help you?"

"I've just popped in to show my face before flying offshore for ya today."

"That's great! Grab a seat. What's ya name, pal?"

"Greedy Twat!" I replied… The office suddenly went very quiet!

Tommy's Tale

It was raining and cold in Manchester. Tommy was at terminal 3 departures, going about the normal routine of checking in for his flight to Aberdeen. There were other flight options open to him, as well as the offer of a free ride up in his mate's motor, but Tommy opted for this flight every time. His choice of flight had nothing to do with the low price or convenience, although for the last 18 months that's exactly what he'd been telling the guys at work.

Once inside the terminal building, Tommy strolled straight up to the 'bag drop' counter and handed over his pre-printed boarding pass and made his way to security.

Nearing the front of the queue, he untied his boot laces and slackened them off; he then slipped his watch into his jacket pocket before taking it off and dropping it into the box for screening along with his boots. He looked on as the travelling amateurs next to him flapped around taking off boots, pulling out laptops and trying to undo belts whilst holding everyone else up.

On the departures board his gate was displayed, so he popped into the gents to check his hair before the final security check and boarding.

Tommy stepped onto the aircraft, and to his relief there was Lucy, his sole reason for opting for this flight. She was a regular hostess on the route, and Tommy had been checking her out for some time now. Sure, there were other travel options but none that featured Lucy. Over the last year and a half, he'd used every opportunity he had to chat to her, and today he'd decided to try his luck and take things to the next level.

In no time at all, the aircraft was pushed off stand, and after a short taxi they were airborne and slowly reaching cruising altitude. The fasten seatbelt light was switched off, and the crew began their rounds serving refreshments to their captive paying customers.

Lucy had passed through the aircraft serving drinks, and Tommy was sure she'd spent a few more minutes chatting to him than anyone else. He was sat on his own in a window seat in the middle of the aircraft, and the two seats on the opposite side of the aisle were empty. Once the aircraft had landed and was well into the taxi to the stand, Lucy stood up from her jump seat, made her way down the aircraft past Tommy and returned to sit in the seat across the aisle from him. She placed a clipboard next to his seat whilst she strapped in and then turned and asked him if he was up for work again. Realising she had remembered him from previous trips, Tommy suddenly felt his face turn a little red with excitement. Flustered, he just nodded his head and smiled.

Unable to get a word out and fearing that he had missed his one moment, he thought quickly on his feet, pulled a piece of paper from his pocket and jotted down his mobile number with *'If you fancy a drink some time, feel free to call me x'* in scruffy print underneath. Tommy slipped the note into her clipboard without her noticing and turned to look out of the window. Lucy stood up, collected her clipboard and made her way to the front of the aircraft ready for arrival at the stand.

The fasten seatbelt light went out, and Tommy stood and made his way towards the exit at the front of the aircraft. Just before exiting, he turned, hoping to get a last glimpse of Lucy, only to find she was right behind him.

"Mr 'Smith' (Tommy's surname), your boarding pass I presume?"

"Oh, errr!" mumbled Tommy as he felt his face go bright red.

"Sorry, but I don't need your phone number, and you may need that," she said, as she handed back his boarding card stub and phone number. "It has the tracking code for your checked-in bag on the back."

Tommy was mortified. This was made worse when a guy

in front turned, and Tommy recognised him from the rig. It was the Team Leader who held the morning meeting at the start of each day. He soon realised that this wasn't going to stay off the radar for long.

Later that day, Tommy headed offshore, and as expected the Team Leader had spread the word in no time. The story had done the rounds of the rig in a flash. Any personnel that hadn't heard it on that first day were captured by the 'and finally' announcement at the morning brief.

That was the last time Tommy flew that route when mobilising. He even opted for a lift home with his mate rather than making use of his return ticket.

Inbetweenie

"The mattresses in the cabins on board our platform were believed to be older than the rig itself! Guys were often complaining of bad backs and a shit night's sleep when sleeping on the beds: like lying on a bag of nuts and bolts.

As with most issues, it often takes an incident before money is spent and changes are made, and our mattress problem was no different. I was nodding off when I heard my roommate clamber into the bunk above. There was the normal crunch and grind of the old springs in his bed as he settled into place.

Seconds later, he must have made an adjustment followed by a strange popping sound coupled with a shriek of pain. I leaped out of bed and asked if he was OK. It transpired that one of the steel springs had popped through the mattress and hooked through his ball bag pinning him to the bed.

I left him in agony and gave the medic a shout in his cabin. He managed to pull himself free, and the puncture wound was patched up, which incidentally bled like a stuck pig. The medic chose not to get very hands-on in patching him up; instead, he offered the required dressing along with supporting advice. He certainly took a hit for the team that night, but we were all fitted out with new mattresses soon after the event!"

CHAPTER 24

Radiography

Radiography is used within the industry to assess the remaining wall thickness of pipework and vessels where corrosion or erosion has affected the integrity of the system. There are several different techniques and systems available on the market, but in general the test part is positioned between the radiation source and the film. The material density and thickness of the item being examined affects the penetration of the radiation and creates absorption or scattering. The differences in absorption are then recorded on the film by way of an image which can then be interpreted to obtain remaining thickness or defects within the material.

The technicians (radiographers) are partially shielded from the radioactive source by the geometry of the equipment during exposure and testing; however, they are also required to remain at a safe distance whilst being shielded by surrounding steelwork and process equipment. A safe exclusion zone is also set up with barriers, warning lights and signs to prevent unauthorised entry into the radioactive area. Radiography testing is therefore generally performed during the night shift as this would have less impact on other work activities that would have to be excluded from the area during the busier day shift.

Radiographers and their assistants (Rad Assist's) regularly monitor the levels of radiation at the safe boundary as well as monitoring their own exposure by wearing Thermoluminescent Dosimeter (TLD) badges that are sent for monthly tests and any dose levels recorded on the individual's record. In addition, those working with radiation are subject to annual health screening and medicals.

Teatime Teaser

Oh, how we wish this one was true, but it's done the rounds that many times it's now believed to be an urban myth... or is it?

Two lads were heading out in the company van to do a radiography job at a terminal. They had all the kit in the van including the radioactive source. En route, they completely forgot about the speed camera. The driver braked too late and clearly saw the double flash of the camera as it clocked his speed and captured an image. Now this wasn't the digital cameras that we know of today. It was the old style with rolls of film that had to be collected and changed by the authorities, then developed and assessed prior to a prosecution.

Both lads in the van knew this. They turned the vehicle around and quickly set up the radiography equipment at the

151

base of the camera. They then positioned themselves at a safe distance behind the van and 'wound out' the radioactive source, sending it down the delivery tube to the camera support. The radioactive scatter would hopefully be powerful enough to wipe the film clean; evidently so, as they didn't receive a speeding ticket. Nor would any of the other drivers who were previously banged to rights on the same roll of film.

Tommy's Tale

Tommy had been working in the company warehouse, as did most new starts who joined the company. Here they could be easily familiarised with the company equipment especially when cleaning and preparing it for storage or re-issue onto the next offshore contract. In time, the base technicians would be trained in inspection techniques and as such serve a form of apprenticeship that would instil well-practised procedures and standards that would be an excellent grounding for a career offshore.

It was another freezing-cold Aberdeen morning, and Tommy was in the warehouse cleaning, counting and checking karabiners. The company had entered one of their six-monthly LOLER (Lifting Operations and Lifting Equipment Regulations) change-out periods. This is when legislation requires all lifting equipment being used by the company to be inspected by a competent person, and as such all the equipment that was in use on the offshore platforms was returned to base and replaced like for like with inspected and certified equipment. A mind-numbing, thankless task, but it was a job. "Hang in there, Tommy," he thought to himself.

When the call came, it was almost as if Tommy's thoughts had been read. The warehouse manager asked him to bob into the office for a chat.

"Right, mate, how do you fancy training as a rad assist?' (Radiographer's Assistant)

'Sign me up!' Tommy said, realising this was his chance to get out on site, and with this would come a pay rise.

"You'll need to do source retrieval training and go for an ionising radiation medical, then we'll get you badged and out on one site by the end of the month. There will be plenty of on-the-job training but we'll get you up to speed in no time."

"Perfect!" Tommy said. He couldn't believe his luck. He headed out of the office with a tape measure he had been given to get an accurate waist measurement for his groin protection device (GPD). He'd been told by one of the lads that it was lead underwear that was worn under the overalls to protect his testicles from any exposure to radiation and as such maintain his sperm count.

A couple of days later, Tommy entered the stores ready for work and was handed a heavy padded envelope marked for his attention. He opened it to find a pair of underpants fashioned from lead squares carefully stitched together by heavyweight fishing line. This was accompanied with a delivery note and a sign-off sheet to be completed by Tommy and the manager.

It was explained to Tommy that he would have to try the GPD on and report to the manager so that the fitting could be signed off by the responsible and competent Radiation Protection Supervisor (RPS) within the company.

Tommy took his parcel into the office toilets and carefully slipped them on over his trousers. They appeared pretty flimsy but then he had been told that this was just a first fit and a far more robust GPD would be manufactured from the sign-off sheet once cleared by the RPS.

Tommy stepped out of the toilets and into the main office to make his way to see the manager. In no time at all, he was greeted by the flash of several cameras and a loud cheer as he stood there in his lead underpants and beetroot-red face… "Ah, bollocks!"

Inbetweenie

"I was assigned to a team of crane mechanics and electricians who were flying out to Italy and then sailing offshore in the Adriatic to perform a five-yearly maintenance scope on an FPSO (Floating Platform Storage and Offloading unit). As the inspector on the team, I was to carry out all of the required Non-Destructive Testing (NDT) and inspections prior to the crane going back into service.

We flew into Italy, and then after an overnight stay headed to the harbour where we boarded a vessel to take us on the three-hour trip out to the FPSO. Once alongside, the only means to get on board was via Billy Pugh. This is a basket that is lowered down to the boat via the crane. It is a large cone-shaped structure with a cargo net stretched around the outside. All bags are placed in the centre of the floor plate ring, and those being transferred stand on the outside on a base plate with their arms crossed in front of them bracing the net. The crane then slowly lifts you from the boat onto the main deck of the FPSO. Helicopter transfer was not an option unless it was an emergency such as a medical evacuation.

The crew on board were generally Croatians who were doing long six-week rotations. It just so happened that they were due to go home at the end of our two-week trip, the day after we were scheduled to put the crane back into service.

As our scope of work neared completion, the crew on board started to get a little twitchy and unsettled as they could see that the crane was still in bits and very much out of service. Every mealtime was spent fending off questions by an increasingly frustrated crew, but the crane engineers kept reassuring them that it would be ready.

Sure enough, the last day came and all of the final checks had been carried out. All that remained was one final inspection by me, and the crane would be signed off for another five years. We had our last lunch on board, and once again a steady stream of crew members passed by our table asking if the crane was ready. The guys assured them that all was good but gestured towards me when they explained that all that had to be done was one final inspection. I finished that meal feeling all eyes on me as the locals murmured between themselves, spreading the word that the English guy still hadn't finished his work.

That afternoon, I carried out an Eddy Current Inspection (ECI) on a weld between the main boom foot pins. This is the main up and down pivot point where the crane boom hinges from. ECI is used to detect surface-breaking cracks around the welds without the need to remove any paint. The paint coatings can actually mask the cracks from visual detection, so it can appear to the naked eye that there isn't an issue. Sure enough, I detected a massive crack. My heart sank. I looked down to see a few of the crew watching me, and for a moment I contemplated telling them everything was fine, but I knew I couldn't do it. In no time at all, my news bombshell spread around the rig, and I was a marked man during dinner that night. One guy looked from his table and ran his thumb accross his throat in a slashing motion.

To my relief, the results were sent for review by a senior engineer at the head office, who downgraded the crane for single-man lifts only. It took a while to lift everybody off one man at a time the next day, but at least everybody made it home for their leave and I escaped with my life!"

CHAPTER 25

The Helicopter Landing Officer

The HLO has a similar role to the Emergency Fire Team Leader that was discussed earlier in that they are responsible for the emergency helideck team. The HLO and the team are trained to deal with more specific emergencies that could potentially occur during helicopter operations. These could include an aircraft engine fire, hard landing, rolled aircraft or even platform evacuation or medical evacuation via helicopters. Although the emergencies relate to aircraft, the range of scenarios that could be thrust upon them requires a lot of training and familiarisation.

In addition to helideck emergency training, the HLOs would also be trained as advanced first aiders and aircraft refuelling and radio communications as well as in the packing and shipping of Dangerous Goods (DGs), which could also include class 7 radioactive materials.

The role of the HLO is generally to give helideck availability to the approaching aircraft as an indicator to the pilots that the deck crew are prepared and liaise with the platform radio operator around flight timings and manifests. The passengers would disembark under the supervision of the Helideck Assistants (HDAs), who would also offload any baggage and freight. All this is carried out under the guidance of the HLO, who supervises the whole operation and has full responsibility and control of everyone on the helideck including the passengers, regardless of their role or seniority when off the helideck and at work.

Teatime Teaser

Our flight had just landed on the helideck, and the HDAs were unloading the aircraft boot and lining the bags up ready for us to collect as we disembarked the aircraft. The HLO didn't look too happy with one of the HDAs and was trying to shout to him over the noise of the rotors that were idling away above their heads. The guy seated next to me commented on what looked like an argument, but I replied saying that to me it just looked like he was trying to be heard over the engine noise. A few seconds later, in full view of the passengers and both pilots, the HLO lifted the HDA's chin with one hand and instantly punched him square in the face. "Nope, that's definitely an argument!" confirmed the guy next to me.

Tommy's Tale

The team had been briefed on the day's activities prior to flying to the satellite platform for the day. The OIM had been informed of any safety and process issues prior to the flight as well as confirming the manning for the day.

At the morning flight briefing the list of guys booked onto the flight was called out along with confirming who was the HLO and HDA's.

The other issue discussed was the weather forecast for the day; particular attention was always paid to the possibilities of low cloud or fog. This particular day was no exception as low cloud was on the forecast from 18:00, but they should have been picked up and flying back to the main complex by then. Nobody wants the fog to roll in and cancel all flying, leaving you stuck on a satellite with nothing but tinned food, no running water and a grotty sleeping bag for the night.

They'd been given the normal assurance from logistics that they would keep an eye on it and lift the aircraft to come and get them if it looked like they could get caught out by the weather. Tommy knew this was bollocks as he'd been stuck plenty of times before after the same assurances.

As per the plan, the guys flew to the satellite in the glorious morning sunshine, and once the helicopter had departed and all had gone quiet, the OIM looked to the horizon and said, "Is it me, or is it all starting to look a little hazy out there?"

"Yep!" said Tommy. "Fucking typical, the fog just waits for

us to land on these shit holes and then it closes in!"

The day rolled by and all the work was done as per the plan. Late afternoon the phone rang and as expected the radio operator in the field gave the OIM their projected pick-up time. In readiness Tommy went up to the helideck and did his checks to ensure everything was in order and safe for the helicopter to land. Meanwhile, the rest of the lads got into their survival suits and carried all the bags and freight up to the helideck.

Due to the weight issues and the amount of freight being flown from the platform, they were going to have to double run the aircraft. This meant Tommy would get four guys into the aircraft along with a stack of freight. The aircraft would taxi them back to the main complex and then return for Tommy, the OIM, HDA's and the last of the guys as well as all the remaining freight.

Tommy had the first aircraft on deck just as the sun was setting although you couldn't quite see it due to the fog and cloud closing in from the horizon. They also lost sight of the main complex lights that were only 10 miles away. Tommy watched as the aircraft hovered, dipped its nose and lifted in the direction of home and then disappeared into the dark gloom.

In no time at all, the fog had closed in all around them, and the OIM soon appeared up at the helideck to check out the situation for himself. Tommy had stayed up there anyway sat in his suit and waiting for the helicopter to return. One of the lads downstairs soon came up to say that the radio op had phoned and the aircraft was about to lift the main complex and head back for them. The fog was sitting very low, and it was as if they were completely encircled with a clear view of the stars above.

One of the lads looked up. "You can land in this," he said.

"So when did you hand in your pilot's licence and opt to be a scaff?"

He was shot down for suddenly sounding like an aviation expert, but deep down everyone actually agreed with him or at least wanted him to be right.

It wasn't long until the aircraft was on approach and Tommy's radio crackled into life with the pilot requesting deck availability. Tommy went through the formalities, and the air-craft continued to slow down and crawl towards them. Not that they could see it; it was just that they could hear it gradually getting louder as it approached. It didn't take long for it to ap-pear in the fog-clear ring above, but rather than lower down towards them, it just hung there.

"For fuck's sake, what's he playing at?" Tommy murmured to himself.

The next thing, they were all lit up by a directional spot-light for a few seconds. Then the spotlight went out, and the helicopter dipped its nose and headed off again.

"Where the fuck is he going now?" said the OIM as he headed down the stairs to get straight on the phone to the radio operator. The RO explained that the pilot thought it was too foggy and he wasn't happy with the visibility.

"Well, you tell that fucker that it isn't that foggy. I can see the moon from here!" screeched the OIM down the phone. He said he would wait at the phone whilst the RO contacted the pilot; he demanded a response.

The pilot actually flew back to the main platform and landed on the deck whilst he waited to see if the fog would lift. In the meantime, the RO relayed the OIM's message to the pilot word for word. The pilot lifted the helicopter again and headed in the direction of the satellite for a final attempt at landing, but he soon decided that it was a nonstarter. The guys including the OIM heard the aircraft buzz over them as it headed back onshore leaving the team stranded for the night. At the same time as he flew over the platform, the RO phoned the OIM with the pilot's response.

"Well, you can tell that fucker that I'm not trying to land on the moon!"

Inbetweenie

"The offshore seagull often be found staring out workers on the North Sea platforms is undoubtedly one of the hardest feathered creatures around, and compared to their much softer seaside resort relatives these look like they are jacked up on steroids!

I remeber one of the guys managing to sneak in a few rays

as he sunbathed out of sight on one of the decks away from the production modules.

When I spotted him, he had clearly dozed off with his T-shirt as a pillow, trying to get some sun on his milky-white torso. I say sleeping because he didn't spot the seagull that was stalking him and taking a shine to the nipple ring that was adorning his man boob.

He certainly noticed the feathered assassin as it attacked like a striking viper, getting a good peck at the ring and stretching his nipple half off. He jumped to his feet like a coiled spring but the seagulls beak had snagged in the ring and it was frantically beating its wings and thrashing around trying to fly free. Meanwhile the once peacefull sunbather was screaming in fright bounding about with the fear of god in him as blood poured from his nipple!"

CHAPTER 26

Internal Inspections

All process and systems on an oil and gas installation need to be inspected for a variety of reasons ranging from safety to functionality and integrity. Equipment that is part of the process, such as pipework, storage tanks, pressure vessels and valves, is periodically inspected. The inspection method chosen is dependent on the information required and the service and construction of the equipment. Engineers also consider the environment and types of corrosion or damage mechanisms that will affect the integrity of the component.

Where possible, equipment is constructed from materials that are resilient to the environment to which they are going to be exposed. For example, carbon steel may be substituted for duplex or stainless steels as these are less susceptible to corrosion and internal erosion. However, this comes at a price as material costs are far more expensive.

From an integrity point of view, equipment can generally be examined whilst in-service. The thickness of process pipework can be determined using ultrasound or radiography. Structural welds can be tested for cracks using a range of techniques including Eddy Current or Magnetic Particle Inspection.

Tanks and pressure vessels can be examined using the aforementioned techniques; however, periodically the vessel would need to be inspected internally and for this the process would need to be shut down, purged, cleaned and made safe for a visual inspection via a confined space, vessel entry.

Where vessels or manifolds require an internal inspection yet they are deemed too small for a technician to enter, then a borescope can be used. There are a whole range of scopes on the market, but generally they come in various lengths with a remote control head unit comprising an integrated video and stills camera with an LED light. Images can be viewed in real time on a display unit or recorded and saved on a memory card to be viewed later.

Teatime Teaser

As Operations Team Leader on the platform, I was very quick to respond when I heard reports of a leak on one of the diesel storage tanks. The environmental impact could potentially be quite serious, so I didn't hesitate in sending one of the process operators to investigate. In no time at all, he phoned to say he'd found quite an aggressive leak and would email through the photographs. The email was with me in no time; so too was the platform manager and the Maintenance Team Leader. Whilst waiting for the email to arrive the OIM also asked me to get the onshore Senior Asset Integrity Engineer on the phone as he'd be the one tasked with making an assessment. It was perfect timing; everyone was stood around my computer, and the onshore team were on the line via conference call just as I opened the email along with the attached image. There on the tank was laid an actual green leek as taken from the fridge in the galley. The operator had used a marker pen to add the image of an angry face… Hence the aggressive 'leek'!

It only took a couple of minutes for the operator's name to be heard over the tannoy system as he was summoned to the office, soon followed by the footsteps of a condemned man entering the OIM's office. I honestly thought the operator was going to be beaten to death by the leek-wielding manager.

Tommy's Tale

It had been a long day mobilising to the hotel in readiness for his flight offshore the following day. The day hadn't been made long by the distance travelled but more by the pain he had developed in his arse. He'd never had piles before, but he suspected that these were what were causing the discomfort in the car and his arse to feel every bump in the road. Tommy had done his best to avoid the poor driving surfaces, but there was always the odd pothole that would catch him out and heighten his concentration.

The issue had come on late into his leave, and Tommy knew he had the option to phone the office, but he didn't want to be turning work down or getting a bad name for himself, so he stuck with the plan. He was flying out the next day to do a few small vessel inspections and found the borescope waiting for him at the hotel reception as he checked in for the night. It was often easier for the companies to get their guys to hand-carry freight than to go through the formal process of shipping it via the warehouse.

After a good soak in the bath to try and ease the pain, Tommy tried to position himself so that he could take a look in the mirror to see what the situation was, but it wasn't to be; he just couldn't get the angle right. Feeling at a loss, he got dressed and headed down for dinner before trying for an early night and a decent sleep. Tomorrow was going to be a long day.

After his steak and chips, he headed back to his room and crashed on the bed to try and get comfortable and watch some TV. Whilst laying there, bollock naked, he reached for his phone and attempted to take a selfie of his arse, but it just wasn't clear enough to see what the hell was going on. Tommy put his phone on the bedside cabinet, and at the same time glanced at the borescope. In no time at all, he had the unit out of its case and fired up ready to go. He pulled a couple of metres of the scope out of the housing and powered it up; the display screen kicked into life, and the light at the camera end was shining nice and bright. He directed the camera at the point of interest and adjusted the camera focus to suit. In no time at all,

Tommy had a crystal-clear image on the screen of his puckered starfish and could easily see the area that was troubling him. Tommy adjusted the image slightly and clicked on 'save image'; whilst he had it set up and zoomed perfectly, he snapped a few more for safekeeping.

On arrival at the platform the next morning, Tommy went to see the medic and explained his situation. The medic wasn't overly keen to stare into his abyss, so when Tommy said he had some photos on his memory stick, the medic opted to use those as supporting evidence for his diagnosis rather than the less appealing smellier alternative.

Tommy received some ointment, and in time the issue was resolved and didn't cause him any further grief. He managed to complete his work and be on his way home after a couple of days offshore. The borescope was left in the hands of the platform, loaded into a container and shipped back to Aberdeen. Now Tommy did say that his piles caused no further problems; well, that is until the inspection equipment provider from where the camera had been rented took receipt of the borescope, and during their sign-off checks they found images on the unit's internal memory. Photos of Tommy's arse-hole were then emailed to his employing company, who were keen to know if he had attempted an internal inspection as well.

Inbetweenie

"I was doing a quick bit of maintenance and inspection on a

system that has a flap valve at waist height. To save messing around with process isolations, you could hold the flap in the open position with a screwdriver whilst you did what had to be done with the air supply turned off. Not good practice in this modern age of health and safety, but back then it was the common-sense approach. That is, until this one day when I turned the air off and realised that I didn't have the required screwdriver, so I held the flap open with my finger. God knows how, but I moved my finger to the point where the flap was wedged and couldn't move and nor could my trapped finger. So there I was, stood in the middle of the process plant area with my hand stuck in a valve unable to reach the air supply valve to release myself.

I had to stand and wait for the right guy to come along who I could trust to set me free without getting me in the shit, not a good situation to be in when it's freezing cold and you're bursting for a pee. Every time a manager or supervisor went past, I made myself look busy and just hoped that they didn't call me over for a chat. I stood there for two and half hours until eventually one of the lads came over and helped me out.

What he didn't realise was that I'd actually given up all hope of making it to a toilet and just peed myself. Thankfully, the thick overalls and layers of clothing hid the tell-tale signs although both rigger boots were part-filled with urine."

CHAPTER 27

Crane Operations

All offshore installations heavily rely on cranes to ensure they can move and transfer much-needed supplies, equipment and in some cases personnel. The crane is without doubt the workhorse of the platform. Should a crane ever be taken out of service for an extended period, it poses huge logistical problems for the platform management. All food and basic day-to-day consumables required for the welfare of the crew are lifted from resupply vessels onto the platform by the cranes. Often the cranes are used to lift the bunkering hoses from the vessels, which then pump much-needed fresh water and diesel from their holding tanks. Virtually each individual platform or installation will have its own crane capable of lifting and positioning equipment, containers and supplies to multiple levels and locations.

In the UK, offshore crane operators are trained to three different stages of competency. A stage 1 course would be for a novice operator with no previous experience and would centre around deck lifts. A stage 2 course would be for an advanced operator and would involve lifting operations over the side of the platform such as to and from resupply vessels. Finally, the stage 3 assessment is to check ongoing competency and would normally be conducted on the platform by an independent assessor who would assess the crane operator during multiple lifts of varying complexity as well as the operator's understanding of planning and coordinating the lifting process.

Cranes tend to have a very robust and in turn heavy hook block at the end of the winch wire rope. In order to protect the deck crew and to ensure loads can be connected to the crane's lifting mechanism safely, a pennant is used as an interim connection. The pennant is the term used in the offshore industry for a single sling leg with a master link at one end that attaches to the crane and a hook at the other to attach to the load. The pennant is much easier and safer for the deck crew to handle and manoeuvre when connecting and disconnecting loads, particularly when on the rolling deck of a resupply vessel.

Teatime Teaser

We had been waiting on the vessel to come alongside the platform so that we could lift off a much-needed production skid for a process upgrade. During lunch the OIM came to my table and asked what time I'd be lifting the skid from the vessel as he wanted to come out and take a look to ensure everything ran smoothly. I told him it was planned for about 14:00. This gave me enough time to get the crane checks complete before every

Tommy, Dick and Harry came out and had a nosey.

After my lunch I headed straight out, fired up the crane, checked my radio comms and completed all of the standard checks. I then placed the boom back in the rest and sat there waiting for the boat to move into position… and that's all I remember!

With a belly full of food, I sat back in the big comfy crane chair and soaked up the sun's warming rays as they shone through the glass canopy of the crane cab. In no time at all I was fast asleep, and out cold! The boat had moved into position, the deck crew were some 30 metres below me on another deck level and the OIM was stood just below my position looking over the handrail at the boat and his highly valued skid.

In the meantime, I continued with my deep sleep, my head slumped to one side party blocking my windpipe, and unbeknownst to me I was snoring like a pig. I was pretty much the only person that didn't know as I had forgotten to turn my radio off and had slumped over onto the transmit button. All around the platform, radio speakers were playing the sound of my snoring to all who were in range. The control room, the deck crew, the supply vessel and worst of all the OIM. The OIM who had climbed the ladder and virtually smashed open the crane cab door.

"Whenever you're ready, twinkle toes!!"

Tommy's Tale

As with most offshore platforms, there was a requirement for those working on board Tommy's rig to wear more than one hat and take on additional roles and responsibilities. Catering personnel would often be seen as advanced first aiders assisting the medic, services personnel could be seen working the helideck as an assistant or helicopter landing officer. Tommy had worked on the platform for a few years as an operator. His primary role was to assist with gas production and all of the associated processes to ensure things ran smoothly and efficiently. Over the past few months, though, Tommy had been asked to assist the deck crew and train as a crane operator and more recently had gone on to complete his level 2 course. He was now qualified to lift and lower loads around the platform unsupervised. Sitting up in the crane cab, towering over everyone, Tommy felt like a pilot who had just received his licence and was free to fly solo for the first time, a position he'd looked forward to for a while.

It was mid-winter, and unsurprisingly the winds were whipping in from the west and blowing hard across the deck of the platform. Tommy was in the control room when he overheard a conversation regarding a lift that was required before the winds picked up to the extent that crane operations would have to be suspended for safety reasons. Without hesitation, Tommy butted in and made his presence along with his newfound qualification known. "I'll jump on the crane and do the lift for ya!" Tommy declared, trying to quash his eagerness and

173

yet assert his availability at the same time.

"Aye, alright… Tie in with the scaffs, and they'll tell you where they need it dropping," replied the maintenance man.

The wind was still whipping up but well within limits for operating the crane, Tommy thought, as he made his way across the lower walkway of the bridge. He toyed with the idea of putting a tannoy out for the 'scaffs' but thought they would soon come to him once they saw the crane boom kick into life and reach for the sky. It's hard to miss so much steel pointing into the air, not to mention the rumble of the crane's diesel engine and the whir of the winch, which can be heard by all on board.

Tommy arrived at the crane pedestal and scaled the ladder to the operator's cab. This was his moment, unsupervised and free to get to grips with the controls without being pestered by one of the old-hand crane ops watching over his shoulder. All throughout his training and mentoring, Tommy had hated being told what to do and corrected for the slightest of errors, not that they were errors in Tommy's eyes. He always said it was like driving a car for your test and how you drive completely differently when you've passed, cutting corners but still a better driver without all the bollocks of doing it by the book.

Now it was Tommy's time to cut corners and do away with all the bullshit. He skipped the full set of pre-use crane checks and just fired up the engine and brought the beast to life. Tommy's aim was to lift the boom vertical and get it up in the air ready for when the 'scaffs' made their way over to sling their load and direct him to the landing area. Without hesitation, Tommy gunned the engine and attempted to lift the boom out of its rest. He had a clear line of sight down the boom and could see the wire rope hanging vertical from the boom tip. The methanol storage tank on the main deck blocked Tommy's view of the pennant attached to the main hook block, but he imagined it to be in its normal place just coiled on the deck and ready for use. As Tommy lifted the boom and it started to rise out of the rest, the cabin was filled with the sound of alarms, indicating that something was wrong. Undeterred by the noise, he just ignored it as a false alarm and continued to force the boom skywards. What Tommy didn't realise was that during the night the pennant had been flapping around in the wind and clattering against the corrugated windwall making a hell of a racket. One of the operators investigated the noise and solved it by wrapping the pennant through the handrails and then clipping the hook back onto the wire, making a secure loop through the railing and putting a stop to all the noise. Tommy continued to ignore the alarms. He watched as the boom suddenly bounced. His heart skipped but then settled again as he watched the boom rise into the air with ease. Out of the corner of his eye, he could see the scaffs were on scene waving at him… All a bit strange, he thought, as the heavily tattooed, shaved headed, knuckle draggers that they are don't normally wave like that. He quickly switched his attention back to the boom and went drip white as he watched a 40-foot section of handrailing slowly rise into the air, spinning like a piece of confetti on the end of the pennant.

Tommy had instantly put his crane operator's career on

hold, compromised the integrity of the main deck safety and cost the company thousands of pounds in repairs.

He had the time it would take to complete the long and lonely walk back across the lower bridge to the control room to work out an excuse to explain his monumental fuck-up, but first he had to descend the ladder from the crane cab to be greeted by a round of applause from the scaffolders who were absolutely pissing themselves with laughter below.

Inbetweenie

"The platform was having issues with blocked drains, and a number of toilets had been taken out of use. I had tried to use the only serviceable toilet a few times during the morning, but every time I went to the cubicle it was 'engaged'; the cubicle next to it had an 'out of order' sign on the door so it was out of action. Finally, the toilet became free and the green vacant indicator was showing in my favour. I settled onto the throne, and after all the patient waiting, I was certainly in no rush. So when there was a knock at the door asking if I was going to be long, I had no hesitation in replying 'it takes as long as it takes' and I carried on reading the newspaper. Not long after, the door was banged on again and the same voice piped up with a little more urgency this time. Again, I replied, but this time with a little more of a 'fuck off and leave me alone' tone about it.

We were at a bit of a stand-off. We both knew who the counterpart was on the opposite side of the door, so, when finally I heard him approach again, this time I pre-empted his plea and told him straight to fuck off and leave me in peace. In all honesty, I could have finished up and vacated but I took pleasure in making him sweat it out for a while.

I heard the cubicle door go next to me and a lot of rustling around. I assumed someone had come to attempt to unblock the drain to get the toilet back into service. Then to my horror the cause of all the noise became apparent when the familiar voice piped up again and said, 'I warned you! Now stick that in the bog when you're done, ya fucker!' At that point, a piece of newspaper was slid under the door carrying a perfectly formed turd. The dirty bastard, I couldn't get out of there quick enough!"

CHAPTER 28

Maritime Operations and Logistics

There is an array of different vessels within the offshore world providing a broad spectrum of services in support of the oil and gas industry. They cover roles including yet not limited to tug operations, surveys, drilling, standby, Search and Rescue (SAR), firefighting, resupply and oil recovery to name but a few. Without such vessels, the exploration, drilling and in turn production from offshore oil and gas installations would simply not be possible.

Fixed installations (oil and gas platforms) rely heavily on resupply vessels to ferry equipment to the platform along with fuel and fresh water. Food is transported offshore in shipping containers, some of which are refrigerated. As full containers are lifted by the platform cranes onto the platform, the previous, now empty containers are lowered back down onto the vessel's deck, commonly referred to as backloading. Often equipment being used for certain projects has to be sent back to 'town', a term used to describe the harbour town nearest to the platform, where the vessels dock to load and offload cargo.

Skippers of such vessels in the past required great skill to hold station alongside the platform, often fighting the swell, current and wind which all combined to make the skipper's job even harder. Modern-day vessels are fitted with a Dynamic Positioning System (DPS), which automatically uses the vessel's own propulsion to maintain a fixed position. Such systems can do little to account for the effect of swell. As containers are lowered towards a vessel's deck, the ships rise and fall on the swell as the containers crash and swing into their final resting place. The whole time during this activity, the vessel's deck crew have to be ever vigilant not to be trapped and crushed by a suspended load. They can be seen to rush in to disconnect a container from the crane's pennant, before guiding it across the deck and hooking it up to the next container. From there, they rush away and stand in one of the pre-designated safe areas before the crane winds in the winch and lifts the next container for transfer free from the vessel's deck.

Resupply vessels are continually making their way to and from the harbour towns and seldom stay within the offshore field for long unless there is a planned logistical requirement or a delay in readying equipment for backload.

Each platform or offshore oil and gas field does, however, have its own dedicated standby vessel. Such vessels are on location to provide emergency cover such as firefighting as well as Search and Rescue. Often a platform will require workers such as scaffolders and Rope Access Technicians to position themselves above the sea, and although these professions have varying safety systems and control measures in place to mitigate the hazards, the potential for a fall to sea has to be considered. As such, all workers are attached to the platform by various kinds of safety lines and anchor points as well as wearing lifejackets, personnel location beacons and in some instances dry suits. Prior to working 'over the side', the standby vessel or one of its Fast Response Craft (FRC) moves within the 500-metre zone of the platform. They would then establish direct communications with the standby man for the team about to work over water and be able to respond within seconds in the unlikely event of a fall to sea.

Teatime Teaser

Radio communications between the pilot of an approaching helicopter and the platform HLO.

All very official and crisp radio transmissions:

Pilot: "XX HLO this is G-XYZ requesting deck availability, please."

HLO: "G-XYZ good morning, sir, XX helideck is available."

The aircraft is on final approach. The nose rises slightly as it flares out into a slow descent. The HLO then looks up…

…Not so official radio transmissions!

HLO: "Put ya landing gear down!"

Pilot: "Ah shit!"

Engines scream out, the nose dips and the helicopter drops away to the side before rising into the air for a second attempt.

…I was the HLO!

Tommy's Tale

The crane boom could be seen slowly slewing outboard over the resupply vessel that was gently rising and falling on the swell. Tommy had made his way onto the deck where the lads were watching the empty container being landed on the container for backload. There's always a flurry of activity as a container is hooked onto the crane's pennant, followed by all eyes turning skyward as it's hoisted into the air before traversing out over the edge of the platform. Tommy watched as the deck crew made their way towards the handrail, all of them stood side by side, arms crossed on the top rail looking down as the crane operator played conkers with the container, clattering it against other units before bouncing it into place on the vessel's wooden deck. This was without doubt a skilled manoeuvre, but it always looked a little precarious to say the least!

"Fuck me, do they actually pay you lot for that?" Tommy said, as the three lads stood motionlessly staring at the spectacle below.

"Aye, they do, pal, more than your lass earns working the streets!" came the harsh but well-deserved retort.

Tommy had spent days winding this crew up, along with

the crane operator. As a young Scouser, he was very quick with the sarcasm and little held him back from having a pop at everyone. Some laughed it off, but others were just waiting for the chance to teach the young lad a lesson, and this deck crew were no exception.

"Why don't ya make yourself useful for a change and clear out the scrap rope that one of your lads has left inside that container with the door open?" said the banksman as he turned and pointed to one of the containers due for backload.

Tommy was no old hand, but he knew that all containers had to be free of loose waste before being put on a vessel and transferred back to town. He headed over and stepped into the container. He was barely through the door when he heard the creak and groan of the door swung shut behind him, soon followed by the 'clunk' of the securing handle as the container was sealed shut. He instantly screamed out and was absolutely petrified as his world went black. Not a single ray of sunlight was able to penetrate the dark void of the steel box that he now found himself in. His fear was compounded as he heard the whir of the crane's winch, and suddenly, he was being thrown to the floor, where he curled up in the darkness. The sound of the whirring winch gradually fell silent as he was lowered onto the boat below, the side-to-side swinging motion replaced by the pitch and roll of the vessel's deck.

Tommy continued to shout in the hope that the deck crew would answer his calls and come to his rescue. It was either that or settle in for the boat ride back to town or potential asphyxiation through lack of oxygen. If daylight can't get in here, surely oxygen can't, Tommy thought as the seriousness of his situation sank in. Tommy sat slumped in the corner, nauseous and scared as he heard the remaining containers one by one crashing into position around him. It seemed like an eternity, but in reality it was about an hour. There was again another crash on the side of his container and he was thrown against the inside wall. He again heard the whir of the platform's crane getting louder but by this time didn't have the sense or perception to understand his situation. His body was rocked with one more jolt as everything again went calm. He heard noise at the door. The clamping handle was disengaged and the door flung open. A flash of light blinded him from seeing the beaming smiles of the deck crew as they struggled to stay on their feet, laughing uncontrollably at the sight of Tommy sitting there like a petrified animal not knowing its fate.

"In future, think twice before you rip the piss out of someone offshore, son, and if you breathe a word of this to anyone, we'll just teach you another lesson… understood?" came the stark warning from the banksmen.

"Aye, understood," replied Tommy.

Inbetweenie

"We had just landed on the platform, and as we disembarked the helicopter, I was the last guy to leave the helideck. The noise from a helicopter's rotors as it ticks over when on the deck is still very loud, so it comes as a shock when you hear a loud bang from its direction. Even more of a shock when you feel something strike you on the shoulder and flash past the side of your face. The guy in front of me turned and shouted 'What the fuck!' as he saw me standing there covered in freckles of blood. I looked beyond him to see one of the guys jokingly attempting CPR on the top half of a seagull that had been cut clean in half trying to fly through the rotors.

It was a bird strike, and thankfully one that we were on the ground for rather than in the air. The helicopter was fine, and after a few checks and clearance from the onshore engineers, it was permitted to continue with its routing. I just had a few spots of dried blood to wash away, but as for the bird, as much as we tried to save it, sadly it was pronounced dead at the scene."

CHAPTER 29

Helideck Safety Standards

The offshore helicopter landing areas (helidecks) on UK in-stallations have to meet very high safety standards as required by the Central Aviation Authority (CAA), the criteria for which is outlined by way of a guidance document (CAP437). Helidecks are subject to inspections and certification by the Helideck Certification Agency. All aspects of the helideck are inspected and tested to ensure they meet the safety standards. These include:

- Helideck equipment such as rescue and firefighting arrangements
- Potential for turbulence created by surrounding struc-tures or vents/exhausts.
- Helideck crew training
- The carriage of Dangerous Goods by air in accor-dance with the International Air Transport Associ-ation (IATA)
- The lighting, landing deck surface area, markings and the levels of anti-slip.

Over the years, the levels of helideck emergency firefighting equipment have evolved from handheld trolleys of foam, carbon dioxide and water jet to automated fire monitors and pop-up sprinkler systems embedded into the deck structure. The helideck crews still have to be prepared for all scenarios from a hard landing to an engine fire, from a medical emergency on board to a full cabin fire. To this end, helideck crews have an array of equipment available to them including Breathing Apparatus, tools and equipment to allow a forced entry through damaged doors and airframes as well as protective fire suits, helmets, visors, gloves and heat-protective flash hoods.

Teatime Teaser

Way back in the early days, we had just started using helicopters to fly offshore. The next development to follow was the introduction of survival suits. These were nothing like the modern-day versions. They were made from a combination of thick foam and rubber with integral boots and mittens. When pressed for feedback, we stressed the obvious difficulties in being able to smoke whilst flying.

The next version was then issued, which allowed you to remove the top half along with the mittens. This would free up your hands and allow you to smoke in the aircraft.

Then came the decision to ban smoking on flights, but as the pilot was seated in a raised position and he was solo, there was nobody to stop us as the pilot couldn't even see the passengers seated below and to his rear!

Finally, the powers that be got wise to this and appointed a steward to attend all flights.

"Who are you?" we asked, as we waited to board the aircraft.

"I'm the flight attendant, here to make sure nobody smokes during the flight."

Within a few minutes of taking off, the flight attendant took a tobacco tin out of his pocket, winked at us and said,

"Stick your fag ends and ash in here, lads."

Tommy's Tale

It was mid-summer and Tommy and Dan were enjoying the Egyptian sun on one of many recent diving holidays. The two weeks on, three weeks off rotation was the perfect mix of work–life balance. Being self-employed in the offshore industry allowed enough time to earn the money required to pay the bills and the taxman but also rewarded you with three weeks off to live life and distance yourself from the offshore world.

Tommy had a passion for SCUBA diving, and with Sharm El-Sheikh on the southern tip of Egypt's Sinai Peninsula only being a five-hour flight away, it was very accessible during a three-week leave period. Diving in the Red Sea has so much to offer after the contrast of two miserable weeks in the cold, wind and rain of the North Sea. On land, the Sinai Peninsula links

Africa with Europe; at its southernmost tip is Ras Moham-
med National Park, which spans an area of 480km² (135km²
of surface land area and 345km² of sea). The area out to sea
is where the currents of the Gulf of Suez to the west and the
Gulf of Aqaba to the east meet, bringing with them a mass of
marine life. For recreational divers there is also easy access to
dive the World War II wreck of SS Thistlegorm as discovered
by Jacques Cousteau or the Abu Nuhas shipwrecks including
Carnatic, Chrisoula K, Giannis D and Kimon M.

Tommy and Dan were in their element diving the warm
waters of the Red Sea by day and drinking the cold beers in the
bars of Sharm El-Sheikh by night. On one particular day, they
had linked up with an English couple who had been diving
together for years and clearly knew their stuff in comparison
to the many other fuds who had all the gear and no idea. You
can easily spot a competent diver in the water in a matter of
minutes and the numpties even more easily!

One evening, after a day of diving, Dan and Tommy met
up with the couple for a few beers… and a few more! The conversation turned from diving to home and in turn to work. Dan
was setting the scene around how daring and wild the offshore
world was and how we needed the break to destress from the
day-to-day risks and danger that we had to continually face…

"What a load of bollocks!" Tommy thought as he heard
Dan laying it on thick. The husband of the couple could see
straight through all the hype, but he went along with it. Dan
then went on to explain how they were also trained firefighters

and worked with helicopters on a daily basis… just falling short of saying that they could fly the things! A few beers later and the husband got in on the act, joking about how his wife had a fireman's calendar in the home office that her sister had given to her.

"That's nothing," Dan replied. "You should see Tommy when he's in his BA kit, fireman's helmet and axe in hand, all silhouetted against the backdrop of a flaming oil fire!"

The laughs rolled on, and the guys enjoyed the rest of their diving holiday before having to head back home and in turn back offshore for another two-week stint. Prior to leaving Egypt, email addresses were exchanged with the normal promises of staying in touch and if ever there was a group dive trip planned, the guys would ensure the couple got an invite.

A week or two later, Tommy and Dan found themselves back at work again on one of the normally unmanned platforms. The sun was shining, it was lunchtime and the rest of the team were sprawled on the main deck eating their sandwiches and catching some rays. Tommy and Dan, on the other hand, were up on the helideck, stripped down to their boxer shorts and topping up their Egyptian tans and joking about the night in the bar and the bullshit Dan had been coming out with. It was then that Tommy had an idea. He headed down to the crash box and donned the BA set and helmet and took the leather sheath from the fire axe. He then made his way back onto the helideck and told Dan to get the camera. By the time Dan returned, Tommy was stood there bollock naked with the mask of the BA set covering his tabernacles… Dan could hardly hold the camera still enough to snap a photo, but snap one he did. There was Tommy, as promised, with everything in the background apart from the huge oil fire. The photo was swiftly transferred from the work camera to a memory stick and secured in Tommy's survival suit pocket ready for the de-man flight back to the main rig that evening. Tommy would then email the photo through to the couple with a brief note about how they may have been pissed, but they weren't bullshitting when it came to being heroes!

That night, Tommy was busy and didn't get the opportunity to get the memory stick from his survival suit, but he knew that he was flying out to work again the next day and would grab it in the morning.

The following day, the guys went through the normal routine of sorting their work equipment ready to be loaded onto the chopper, then grabbed their lunch bags that had been prepared by the night steward before attending the flight safety briefing. From there, the team went down to the muster point on the platform and grabbed their survival suits from the racks, where each person had an allocated storage area for their issued suit. Tommy was in a rush and grabbed his suit, before climbing the stairs to make his way up to the heli-lounge and waiting for the flight. On arrival at the satellite platform, Dan reminded Tommy of the memory stick. Tommy instantly put his hand into the pocket of his suit, and to his disbelief the stick was missing. His world fell apart. Where the fuck had that gone and, more importantly, who the fuck was going to find it?!! Tommy looked again at the suit and soon realised that it wasn't his. In the rush to get ready, Tommy had grabbed the wrong suit and his cabin mate must have had his… His cabin mate, who would actually be flying home later that day and was sure to find it! His cabin mate, who was also one of the managers, and who wouldn't be able to resist looking at its contents! His cabin mate, who was also a company man, and who would undoubtably get Tommy sacked for fucking about with safety equipment!… Tommy's arse fell out, and Dan couldn't stop laughing, which obviously didn't help the situation!!

After a while, Dan calmed Tommy down and they hatched a plan. Tommy phoned the recipient of the memory stick and explained that he had mistakenly taken the wrong survival suit. Tommy also went on to say that there was a memory stick in the pocket of the suit that he had left behind and could it please be handed into the control room for him to collect later that evening. Tommy then played his trump card and said that the memory stick contained a virus and under no circumstances should it be plugged into a computer… Genius!

That evening, Tommy returned to the rig and headed straight to the control room. The lads there handed him an envelope which had been left by the manager, who had headed home earlier that day. Tommy felt the world lift from his shoulders as the envelope was handed over and he could feel the memory stick safely secured within. Walking away from the control room and into the recreation room, he made himself a cuppa before sitting down, tearing open the envelope and taking out the memory stick, around which was wrapped a yellow Post-it note…

'NICE AXE… SEEYA IN 3 WEEKS!'

Inbetweenie

"The senior steward decided to prank one of his lads by saying that he had received a complaint about a turd that had been left in the manager's toilet and the assumption was made that it was the young steward who had left it there whilst he was in cleaning the cabin. The plan was that a chocolate bar would be rolled in someone's warm hands before being slipped into the u-bend. After being submerged in the toilet water for a while, it would go a little furry at the edges and take on the appearance of a wee jobby. The supervisor would then get the accused to attend the cabin toilet and ask him if he knew anything of the offending article and how it got there. The joke would then be driven home by the supervisor, who would reach into the toilet and pull it out with his bare hand to present the evidence to the poor steward. The success of the prank would be measured by the reaction of the young lad's face as a dummy turd is wafted under his nose.

In this case, however, everyone was in on the joke including the 'accused' young lad; everyone, that is, except for the senior steward. Chocolate wasn't used to facilitate the gag. In fact, the guy tasked with positioning the chocolate bar dropped his trousers and pushed out the genuine article.

The senior steward was left with egg on his face… and shit on his fingers!"

<u>Abbreviations</u>

AD	Assistant Driller
BA	Breathing Apparatus
BOSIET	Basic Offshore Safety Induction and Emergency Training
CRO	Control Room Operator
DGs	Dangerous Goods
EBS	Emergency Breathing System
ECC	Emergency Control Centre
ECI	Eddy Current Inspection
ECITB	Engineering Construction Industry Training Board
ESD	Emergency Shutdown
FPSO	Floating Production Storage Offloading
FRC	Fast Rescue Craft
HDA	Helideck Assistant
HLO	Helicopter Landing Officer
HSE	Health and Safety Executive
HSEQ	Health, Safety, Environment & Quality
IRATA	Industrial Rope Access Trade Association

MACP	Manual Alarm Call Point
NDT	Non-Destructive Testing
NUI	Normally Unmanned Installation
O&G	Oil and Gas
OETL	Offshore Emergency Team Leader
OETM	Offshore Emergency Team Member
OIM	Offshore Installation Manager
OPITO	Offshore Petroleum Industry Training Organisation
PAPA	Prepare to Abandon Platform Alarm
PLB	Personal Locator Beacon
POB	Personnel on Board
PPE	Personnel Protective Equipment
RAT	Rope Access Technician
RPS	Radiation Protection Supervisor
SAR	Search and Rescue
SBC	Small Bore Connection
TL	Team Leader
TLD	Thermoluminescent Dosimeter
TRA	Temporary Refuge Area
UKCS	United Kingdom Continental Shelf
VIP	Very Important Person

Printed in Great Britain
by Amazon